REVENGE &
PERSEVERANCE
By
Lynne Adams Barze'

Author and publisher - Lynne Adams Barze'

Technical Advisor – Theodore H. Barze' Jr.

Editor – William R. Jackson

Illustrations from 123RF

DEDICATION

I was always a star in her vision,
To nurture us best was her mission.

She knew what we could grow to be,
And wanted the rest of the world to see.

When I looked in a mirror and wondered what
I'd be,
Only beauty, intelligence, and success she could
see.

So no one else could I ever dedicate to,
But my mother, Dear Audrey, this book was
done for you.

Lynne Adams Barze' , 2014

REVENGE & PERSEVERANCE
By
Lynne Adams Barze'

FROM UNDER THE PORCH

I was playing outside behind the storage building. On the weekends I stayed at my Granda's house because my dad worked extra days on a second job. He said we needed more money since Mama was gone to cover all we needed to pay on each month. He said living on one paycheck was harder than living on two. Mama was gone and so was her paycheck, but all of her bills weren't. He said that Uncle Eddy, who he'd thought was his friend, had two paychecks now, though, with Mama's help.

I was getting real hungry because when I got up that Sunday morning, Granda wasn't in the kitchen making breakfast. Now it was after 12:30. I heard the front gate creek open very slowly so I started walking out toward the front of the house. It was Gramp but he just didn't look right. For one thing, he looked dirty, like he had been standing out on the edge of a busy, dusty road. He was carrying something over his shoulder like he might carry a sack of vegetables or something but it looked a bit longer than the biggest sack I had ever seen.

For some reason I started getting scared, real scared and I didn't understand why. It was only my Gramp. But I had never seen his face look so dark and angry, so I ducked under the front porch before he could see me. I laid there very quiet looking up through the cracks in the old wood. Then something dripped through the cracks right on to my forehead and it didn't smell very good. It reminded me of the time we found that dead armadillo in the gutter up the road, but worse. My dad said it had been hit by a vehicle and had been dead for some time. That's how the whole air smelled, like something had been dead for some time. I saw something drag across the crack in the porch floor. It was Granda's slipper on her right foot, her left one was bare. Gramp was carrying Granda. Was she sick?

I heard one of the wooden kitchen chairs scrape across the floor and then a smothered whoop sound as if something was plopped down into the chair. And I heard my Gramp's voice, but not quite his voice. The voice was a sort of groaning, guttural, moaning sound. Yet it was like words were trying to come out, too. Then it seemed that whatever had been put into the chair fell out of the chair onto the floor, hard and I heard the chair tip over real loud. I heard Gramp's voice howling. He started stomping his feet and pounding his fists against the wall. And the smell grew worse.

Daddy got off work earlier on Sundays, so just about then I heard his truck pull into the drive. I was so relieved to know he was home. I scrambled out from under the porch and ran crying, flailing my arms and yelling, "Get back, get back! Something's wrong in Granda's house. Help, help, Daddy, help!"

Daddy got out of his truck with his over and under shot gun in his hands. He ran past me and went right up the porch steps and stormed into Granda's front door. I heard yelling and cussing and growling as if my dad had come face to face with a wild animal. Then I heard the shots - once, twice, then a third time. The smell of the cordite mixed with what I had smelled from under the porch.

Dad ran back out of the house, held me close, and walked me back toward his truck. He called Sheriff Connelly and told him to bring Father Dean from St.

Monica's Church to my grandparent's house. Then he said something else that shook my young world, he said the "Zombi Flu" had struck our family and that he would get the wood fire ready.

BOOKS

Zombi Flu

It had been seven days since I heard the term "Zombi Flu" and my dad had gathered the large fallen oak tree and gasoline to make the big fire. I didn't understand any of it for a while. Why was my daddy angry one minute and crying the next. Why didn't he want me to leave his side? Why couldn't I go to school? My father had always been so big and strong, but now he seemed to shrink and weaken. His rifle never left his hand. He topped off the gas tank in the truck every other day. I was scared - for him.

When the sheriff had gotten to my Granda's property that day, he had brought Deputy Clark and Deputy Steve with him. They didn't need to talk with my dad; they seemed to know why they had to go into the house. In a short time, they came out struggling with an enormous bundle that looked like something rolled up in Granda's living room rug. I didn't know what that could have been, but I know I never saw Gramp or Granda leave the old house and I have never seen them since, either.

The giant awkward bundle was carried over to the, by then, fierce raging wood fire. With great effort and difficulty, the three lawmen tossed it right into the middle of all the flames. There was a whoosh of embers and black smoke. Soon the fire ate into the bundle then the most awful odor filled the air, yet that wasn't the worst thing to happen. Cries of pain and rages of anger began rising from the terrible scene in front of me.

My father and the three lawmen pumped buckshot into the morass over and over again until their double barreled weapons and supply belts were exhausted. The voices stopped, the fire continued to do its work and the low overhead clouds reflected the glow of the carnage down below. My dad took me home, but the sheriff said the deputies would stand guard until there was nothing left but ashes. Father Dean had brought a fifty gallon drum of water that he had blessed on Holy Saturday. He stayed to pour this over the ashes to wash them into the ground.

My father and I returned to the property in the early morning. There was a crew waiting with a bull dozer and a back hoe. Even though there hadn't been any other activity on the property, Dad was having every structure standing that could hold any memory of the recent horrid past within it brought to the ground and the materials they were built from buried.

It was discovered that my Gramp had spent the early days with symptoms of the Zombi Flu holed up in the tack room of the barn. From what was found there, Granda thought she could help him with old world herbs and cures. They had married in their teens and loved each other for the last fifty-seven years. It was no wonder why she tried so hard not to let him go. But this flu was like no other the world had treated before and ultimately it brought disaster to them both.

Daddy said he would let the land "lay waste". I didn't know exactly what that meant, but by all indications it wasn't very good.

On the way back home, we stopped by the sheriff station. He was still trying to track down how my Gramp had gotten infected. Three other cases had shown up in our county, but no one could find a connection between the infected victims. And just like in the case of Gramp and Granda, each infected victim had killed or infected someone else close to them or in their individual families. It was time to find out if other towns were involved. It was time to admit that we needed help. But would anyone who could help believe in the problem that we had?

The town of Chatawa was about forty miles away in the same county. The Morgan's lived on a large lot of almost a half-acre just before the first subdivision outside of town to the west. Mrs. Morgan had called in sick to her job for the last three days and refused to leave her bedroom. Glen Morgan had been out of town for work, so the kids fixed themselves frozen dinners and ham sandwiches. However, that supply was running low with two active teenagers who played soccer after school and their mom still wouldn't come out of her room but just moaned when they knocked on the locked door. Mat and Allie were really glad to see the taxi pull up with their dad from the airport.

"Dad, we're starving and Mama won't come out", was the first thing to burst from Mat's mouth.

"Dad, it's not that critical, but Mat's right." admitted Allie. "We haven't seen Mama in days. She won't talk to us. She just keeps moaning like she's angry or something."

Their dad looked at them as if they were making it all up. He gave them each a big hug after setting his luggage in the hall closet. It was his habit since his wife hated clutter. He would unpack later. He headed up the stairs.

When he got to the top of the flight, he turned to look back downstairs at the kids and asked, "What is that smell? Did you guys start another science project or something?" The kids just threw their hands up and wagged their heads no.

Mr. Morgan tapped lightly on the bedroom door. If his wife was having her monthly discomforts, he

13

didn't want to make the mood any worse than it was. But just as the kids reported, his tap was only greeted with a guttural reply. He had carried a skeleton key on his key ring that was keyed to all of the inside doors since the kids were toddlers and he used it to enter the master bedroom.

Just as he entered, he glimpsed a figure scoot into the en-suite bath. He noticed something else, too. The stench in here grew stronger and reminded him of spoiled meat. Remembering what the kids said about his wife not leaving the room for anything the past few days, he thought it might be discarded used feminine products in the bedroom trash can. He decided to just take the kids out for pizza and let his wife rest.

When they returned home with full tummies of pizza and ice cream, Allie and Mat went to do homework in their rooms. Glen sat in front of the TV to watch his favorite 9pm cop show. He'd decided to unpack in the guest room and shower in the hall bath later not to disturb his wife. It had been an exceptionally long day and he soon fell to sleep. The sofa backed to the foyer and Glen didn't hear his wife descend the front staircase.

Suddenly Glen was startled wide awake by an excruciating pain and tugging and growling as something clamped on to the back of his neck. And the stench that filled the air was totally nauseating. He desperately reached behind himself to grab the horrid attacker in any way he could. "What kind of animal could this be?" is what traveled through his mind during the torturing pain. He felt head, shoulders, and arms reaching for his hair. "Human? Could this be a human? But How?"

"Daddy, Daddy! Mommy, no, no!" It was Allie screaming from the top of the stairs. Then Glen was released, the front door was thrown open so hard that the knob got stuck in the sheetrock wall and Alice Morgan ran screaming, growling into the night. Lights were coming on in neighboring homes and approaching sirens could be heard.

Someone had dialed 911 and Mat was calling for paramedics while Allie was rushing to get towels to hold against her father's ravaged neck.

Thirty minutes later Mr. Morgan was being questioned by the police. The ambulance was waiting to transport him to Capitol General Hospital a few miles away. He had been bandaged and the bleeding stopped, but the wound still had to be cleaned and he needed shots, lots of shots.

The policeman was saying, "Sir, your daughter says it was your wife that she saw biting you on your neck. Isn't that right?" Glen tried hard to lessen suspicion on his wife until he could get to the bottom of exactly what was going on. After all, he hadn't really seen who or what it was that had bit him. "Well Officer, are you trying to say my wife thought I had a pack of wieners on my neck, Sir?" The attempt to lighten the seriousness of the situation and take the attention off of his wife went right over the strictly business officer's head. He was about to continue the interrogation when he received an urgent call from his commander.

It seemed that, from a 911 call, a "wild woman in night clothes" had run onto the highway and was struck by a truck. The officer said he would expect Mr. Morgan to come downtown to give a statement the next day and rushed off with his partner.

The paramedic wanted Glen to get into the ambulance to take better care of the grave wound at the back of his neck and he lifted the temporary bandage that had been applied earlier in order for another officer to make his report. He got out his flashlight to see better and was shocked by what he saw. The large, ragged,

15

gaping bite that was previously bleeding and oozing thick drainage was little more than a red swollen scratch. He called his partner over, but it was decided that like most head wounds, this one must have bled worse than it really was. What other answer could explain such rapid healing? And what was that slight stench coming off of the gauze?

Mr. Morgan was feeling great so he talked his way out of the ride to the hospital and promised he'd get the shots they advised and thanked the EMTs for their help. Since Mat and Allie had gone home with their grandparents, his next concern was finding his wife. After changing to clean street clothes, he took his car through the neighborhood. It didn't bother him at all that he felt no pain or discomfort from his neck.

He needed to be first to find his wife. Nothing and no one else mattered now or ever would again. Once he joined her they would eat together and then they would share their anger.

When the police officers got to the traffic accident, they were given a clearer report of the scene. Traffic was stopped for a mile before the accident where the traffic unit was diverting vehicles off at the previous exit. Bright lights were positioned all around the area of attention. A woman in a filthy nightgown had run howling and wailing right into the path of an eighteen wheeler. The scene was utter chaos. Onlookers were staring, crying, and even throwing up. The sounds in the air were horrific, but the smells were far worse than any of these.

Because the two officers were on the scene of what appeared to be a related report, they were ushered into the foray by the first-on-scene officers at this location. No one could absorb what was unfolding before their eyes.

The truck driver had tried to stop in time, but the haste of the impact prevented avoidance. The truck wasn't able to stop until after the first four wheels of the eighteen wheeler rolled over the woman and she laid under the mid wheels of the tractor. Everything was put on hold until the right size tow truck and jacks could arrive. As sad as this would ordinarily be, it was far from the horror that made this such an exceptional sight.

The body of the woman in the filthy nightgown was moving. As screams of anger were coming from her mouth, a gagging odor rose from her breath. The hot bright lights seemed to make it all so much worse. It smelled like someone was cooking rotted meat on a searing flame. Her eyes were open; her fists were pounding the asphalt. She wasn't showing signs of pain, but of hate and rage.

A car sped onto the scene from the east bound lane and screeched to a stop. A man jumped out and raced to the scene in a stumbling, wobbling manner. His clothes were disheveled, his hair a mess, his expression pure outrage. Before anyone could react, he was at the accident victim's side holding both her hands. Then as if the scene couldn't get more horrific, he began to pull her from under the wheels of the massive truck.

There were sounds of snapping, popping, squishing and then a final whoop as the upper torso of the woman broke free from the rest of her that was still pinned under the huge tires. There was no scream of pain or resistance to the man's grip. The man cradled his prize like a young child in his arms. The woman seemed to be urging him on to yells of, "Hurry, hurry, hurry!"

No one could understand what was happening or seemed to know what to do. Not the county deputies, not the emergency response people, not the on-lookers, not the truck driver who was now kneeling on the ground ripping handfuls of hair from his bushy head.

Finally one of the approaching officers yelled, "Stop! State Police! Stop or I'll shoot!" And then he did with an over and under shotgun. My daddy shot again and again and ordered his men to do the same. He was the only one who knew what they were up against and what they had to do.

Every civilian vehicle and all on-lookers were moved back a half mile before anything else could be witnessed.

My dad ordered the officers to get shovels from the trunks of their squad cars and when the massive tow truck lifted the tractor, with gloved hands, they collected every particle of the couple from the asphalt and the truck tires. All of this, along with the messy shovels were deposited into the car that the man had driven up in and it was loaded onto a flatbed. The entire package was then taken out to a field on state property and set ablaze until the car was nothing but scorched metal. Then it was all buried and drenched in holy water and under six feet of dirt.

The virus was spreading and still nobody knew how. The county wasn't that large - 150 square miles. The main four lane highway traveling east to west, only two-lane roads moved north to south. Yet the people in the known cases seemed to share no familial or work related connection.

There was the young woman who inherited her family's vintage book store, in perfect health when she moved to Chatawa to keep it open in their memory. Two weeks later she was found dying in the bedroom of their rear apartment. The authorities had been called there by customers with complaints of a smell at the door.

After her apparent death, she was put into the hospital freezer to retard the rapid decay that was attacking her remains until next of kin could be found. Later when the virus was identified, she was thawed and cremated. Her ashes were dissolved in Holy Water then poured down the sacristy drain at St. Monica's.

Next there was the taxi driver in Howardsville who took his last fare to the middle of a corn field and lived in his car until he consumed his passengers to the bone. Surprisingly, his log book evidenced that this only took thirty-six hours. Only the sharp blades of the farmer's combine prevented him from inflicting further harm in the farming community. But even that wasn't as final as first thought. When the cabby's mangled body was seen wobbling down the medical clinic basement hallway, the night watchman emptied all 16 rounds of his 9mm into his rotting face.

St. Monica's pastor had been summoned to the ER for an accident victim who was dying from his injuries, when he was drawn to the commotion. If he hadn't been there, this small township would have had no idea how to stop any of the infected ones or their victims from spreading more infection.

It had been sad to see the free standing Book Store building at the entrance to the small downtown business district so dark and empty at mid-morning of a typical working day. Two regular customers had gotten out of their cars to speculate on the future of "READING FOR THE FUTURE BOOKS & PERIODICALS" whose motto had been "Good reads sow good seeds." So few stores like this were left and the daughter's return to town had held so much promise. Just last week both their grandchildren had come home from the class field trip all excited about the fantastic "vintage" books they had held in their own little hands. They were even amazed at how funny real cotton fiber paper and leather covers felt and organic glue smelled. Where would they get such old-school lessons now?

A stranger walked up with a coffee in his hand. He told the ladies that he had gone to the coffee shop while he waited for some activity at the shop. He said he'd been invited to town to appraise three volumes that the shop owner had found in a vault in the basement floor. She'd told him that the books seemed ancient, were leather bound and written in an old language. He was both anxious and excited to get his hands on them and may even be interested in making an offer for them. He said he had been laid up with a sinus infection for the last two weeks and hoped the delay hadn't threatened his chance to be the first to appraise them. The bewildered customers suggested he talk to the sheriff and told him where the county offices were located.

However, when he got there, the sheriff and all of his deputies were out of the office. The receptionist would only say that all hands were on a call at the school bus barn. He would have to wait to talk to Sarah's next-of-kin who was due in that night.

All of the school board facilities management departments were housed in large buildings on a fifteen acre site out on Ray Meyers Road. Ray Meyers had been the first Public Works Supervisor and had held the position for twenty-five years. His house was on the first half acre lot carved out of the old Carver farm which was divided up and sold in parcels over the years.

The school security staff had cleared everyone out of their work spaces and roped off the road. Everyone's attention was focused on the school bus barn. The deputy said there was only one bus in the barn. She said that the entire third and fourth grade classes, the driver, two teachers and an aid were on board that bus.

20

The huge double doors at the front and back of the barn and the storage loft doors were wide open. No sounds could be heard, but when the wind blew, the odor that came downwind toward the curious crowd, sent most people running for their cars and rolling up their windows.

Some people tried to leave, but the state police cruisers were arriving by then and told everyone by PA system that they were going to be interviewed. The relatives of those in the barn were separated from the school system personnel and moved back a little up the road.

Miss Ellen, the fifth grade teacher, had gathered all the students that had gone on the bookstore field trip in Chatawa. The twenty-three children, the sixth grade teacher, Miss Sheila, and the teacher's aide, Charlotte, got on the school bus before 6am with Angela, the regular driver who had been out sick the day of the original outing. Charlotte substituted as a school bus driver in Howardsville so she easily handled the driving that day.

Miss Ellen and Miss Sheila had dark circles under their eyes and looked really tired, Charlotte was sweating like she had a fever, but the ladies all insisted they were up to this special outing and the children would not take no for an answer. They were dressed and on the bus faster than their folks had ever seen before. Though they seemed a little awkward and off balance, the parents just figured it was because they were still "sleepy heads."

The teachers said the students didn't need money or lunch and that the permit slips on file were sufficient for this trip as well. It was all done in a bit of a rush, but no one doubted the word of the respected teachers or friendly aid.

21

Angela and her family had transferred to the county in the last month. She had driven school buses for the last fifteen years and fully trusted the loyal teachers and never doubted the call from Miss Sheila for the unscheduled field trip. Besides, she hadn't been to the old book store yet and she loved vintage text.

All of that had started more than nine hours ago. No one was aware that anything was wrong until the school bus load of children and women hadn't returned to the elementary school by lunchtime - first or second schedule. Then the public works people started reporting that they couldn't get access into the #3 bus barn on Ray Myers Road. They also reported a foul smell and a woman's agonizing screams. That's when all hell broke loose.

As soon as the report came over the radio, my dad sounded the emergency alert. State troopers, county deputies and town sheriffs and EMT's from our county and those north and south of the lines responded and soon began arriving and receiving orders from the upper ranking officials of Carverland County. Everyone was whispering about what no one wanted to admit - "Zombi Flu." After the recent occurrences, county fathers from sixty miles around had held meetings in secret with medical experts in an effort to squelch this spreading decease and pin point its origin and a common denominator among the victims.

Parents began showing up in cars, trucks, and SUV's. Some had to be physically restrained, others sedated. Some had heard about the incidents taking place around the area. The local radio station van was the first media to arrive. There was not going to be a chance of keeping the lid on the happenings in Carverland County much longer.

By this time, Dad and the other officers were straining to peer into the barn through binoculars. It was

22

still daylight, but the bus barn interior was getting very dark even with the doors and windows flung open. The large hot lights had just arrived and would soon turn the entire seen into bright white light. But why was the scene so still. The reported anguished cries of the woman had stopped four hours ago. Then the snarls and growls began with yelps and screams that seemed to come from adult and young voices. And there were knocks like small boulders being slammed against the bus floor and even the walls. Some windows were broken out from the inside as bodies seemed to be thrown against them.

Besides the snaps and pops that everyone was afraid to try and identify there was also an awful squishing sound like someone walking or sliding in melting snow, but the month of April had no snow at all that year. And snow could never carry that smell unless it was melting over a rotting corpse.

My daddy was so scared for me that he would not leave me be anywhere he wasn't, but to this day I feel he caused me more harm than he ever meant to. He tried to keep me from seeing the worst of things while keeping me safe but as they say, "Little pictures have big ears." He left me lying on the back seat of his locked state trooper squad car and ordered me to keep my eyes closed until he returned. And without seeing the horrors the others saw on that evening, yet hearing the terrible words and phrases and exclamations and descriptions of what was seen and what had been done and what was about to be done, I wished the Lord had made me born deaf and dumb.

Someone shouted, "The door, the door of the school bus is openin'!"

"Who is, what is that comin' out the door?" said another, "Oh my God it fell! It's missin' half a leg! HALF! What could'a done that in that bus?"

23

The chief of police from the state capitol had a driver bring another bus around. All of the parents and relatives of those believed to be on the suspicious school bus were gathered from the place where they'd been waiting with the on-lookers and put under protective custody on the police bus and taken back to the county offices by one of the officers. They were all in such a state of shock by then that little resistance was offered.

From where I was in my dad's squad car, I heard that another individual left the bus and stumbled over the struggling creature on the ground. They shouted that a third one jumped right on top of the first and began gouging and ripping away flesh or the blackened substance that supposedly had been flesh. The civil defense personnel began handing out gas masks in case the virus was air born and that helped with the stench as well. Everyone on the scene knew what was going on but no one wanted to think beyond the instant time frame they were in.

The "women" that had come off of the bus were pumped with lead from head to toe until they stopped moving and howling. The men who volunteered to climb up into the school bus were seasoned lawmen, but they left the area in hysterics and tears. My dad went in and when he came out he stood in the yard, looked up to the sky, and screamed to the top of his lungs but not in rage or hatred, but in shear agony and tears.

The local newspaper reporter had arrived a short time after the radio station crew. One of the troopers brought the photographer over to the barn, handed him a mask, and asked him to photograph every inch of the scene - in and out of the bus, around and under, and all points of the barn. The man was a seasoned journalist who had photographed everything from wars to train wrecks and duly completed his assignment then vomited into his mask and passed out in the dirt.

24

All of this was being clearly reported by the news people within earshot of where my dad had stored me for safe keeping. And I was a perfect "little picture" with excellent hearing. As I said, I was sorry I wasn't afflicted with poor hearing.

Only one father out of all of the parents of the twenty-three children who had gone on the field trip had been allowed to remain at the scene. Mr. Allen Harper was a county district attorney and a well-respected pillar of the community. The officials felt his word would be honored by the rest of the county when word was reported about what was about to be done and needed to be done. He was shown the pictures and personally spoke with the photographer and officers who had entered the bus. He was offered the opportunity to look in the school bus for himself and given the reports from the other occurrences to read. After Allen Harper regained his composure, he agreed to what obviously had to be done to the remains inside the barn and the school board agreed to what would become of the barn itself.

Army personnel trained in the use of flame throwers had been ordered on to the scene. Military personnel didn't need any explanation to follow orders and after all safety precautions had been taken, the blaze was set. The old country barn itself was made of quarter sawn boards and had been built in the 1920's. It was one of the few original Carver Farm buildings left and still in good shape. It was a pity to loose such a fine historical old structure, but unfortunately quite necessary.

At 7am the next morning, three fire department tanker trucks from the Yotashi County Fire Department arrived and Fr. Dean performed a massive blessing of the water inside the tanks. The fire was allowed to burn to the ground and the embers were extinguished with the Holy Water. Bulldozers were brought up from

25

neighboring communities and the immense task of burying the charred metal bus and ashes - both organic and inorganic - began. The entire effort would eventually take four days, but the bigger effort of talking to, comforting, and soothing the relatives of the victims - children and adults - would be an even larger job.

The county officials, state trooper commander, my dad, Fr. Dean, the photographer, and DA Harper got into cars and headed downtown. Even though they were on the scene, heard the sounds, and smelled the air at the bus barn facility, it was going to be difficult to explain to many of these relatives why the entourage was not arriving with their children and loved ones.

The photographer had called ahead and forwarded the images he'd taken to the chief editor. Someone from the newspaper met them with a sealed envelope containing three albums of printed images from the crime scene. If words hadn't convinced them of the fact that the officials had done what had to be done and all that could be done for the sake of the living with the remains and that remains were all that was left of their loved ones, there was no estimate how this incident would have ended. But pictures speak louder than words and those who had the courage to view the pictures had no more words.

But the family members had not been left alone. They had been counseled by clergy and psychologists who had been waiting for them when they arrived at the county building. Word had gotten out about the tragic losses and that serious help would be needed and they hadn't hesitated to volunteer their training. Some of them had taken part in extended sessions after the high level meetings of the officials in charge in case any more of the virus broke out in the community.

So by the time the officials arrived, most of the hysterics were contained and a numb quiet had settled

26

over the group. No one needed to view any more pictures, but they were adamant that these prints never be released to the public. The sheriff put all three binders into his office safe at the time in case they would be needed in court later. They have all been destroyed since.

My daddy was still the main man on the case. He was temporarily reassigned to the special task force organized for the case and unanimously voted Task Force Leader. The first thing on their list of duties was identifying the common source of the virus that infected so many people from so wide an area across the county. Because the victims had a history of not dying unless shot in the head and then burned to ash, there weren't any autopsy reports to compare. Even the ashes weren't available for analysis because of the dowsing with Holy Water and unorthodox burials. So it was necessary to produce social and financial forensic autopsies.

Again, I was being introduced to terms and behavior I may not have ordinarily been aware of for years to come. But there was no time to wait to grow up. Knowing everything and everyone was what was helping to keep me and Daddy alive and uninfected.

All of the victims' names were placed across the top row of a big white board on the wall of the huge room the officers referred to as their "call room". The children though were only listed as "5th Grade Class" and "6th Grade Class"; they also listed the five kids who stayed home from class that day.

The other victims were posted in the order in which their infection became evident. Under each picture was posted a sheet with a statement from the nearest relative's recollection of his or her activities in the last two weeks of their lives. It had been decided by medical staff, from eye witness reports of those who had most recently seen the victims that two weeks was about the best guess for an incubation period of the virus.

The sequence of infected lined up like this:

1. Sarah Good - heir to the vintage book store
2. Roger Spinner - taxi driver
3. Gramp -
4. Alice Morgan - president of her book club
5. Miss Ellen, Miss Sheila, Charlotte - Eddy Carver Elementary School employees
6. 5th & 6th graders - school attendees
7. Five children not on original field trip - victims in barn
8. Angela - regular bus driver, off sick on day of original field trip - victim in barn

It was the general thought that Angela Hinkley, who hadn't gone on the original field trip, was the victim of an attack by the infected ones and it was her they had heard screaming in agony from the bus barn.

From the next-of-kin statements the team was able to connect everyone except Gramp to the book store. Since I was confined to being my dad's sidekick, I had made a serious effort to stay out of the way. However, I tugged on his sleeve when I realized I had something helpful to contribute. I reminded my dad about the first edition Mark Twain novel that Gramp had given Granda for their 57th anniversary and that he had found it at "Reading for the Future Books & Periodicals." That made the whole room go very quiet. That last connection seemed to complete the circle of infection with the vintage book store right in the middle.

But that still didn't pin point the immediate source of the virus, only the building that may be housing it. A lot of detecting remained to be done and it would start by talking to Hank Good's sister who was due into town the next day. The officers didn't know if she would know about the recent activities around the store, but she could give them permission to search the premises and remove any suspicious or contaminated item or items. Also, no one had a clue what they would be looking for at that point.

When my dad and four members of the task force arrived at the vintage book store, the appraiser who had been invited to look at the three volumes from the basement floor safe was just leaving with his briefcase. The lawmen had no idea who he was, so no effort was made to question or detain him. Inside the store they found a very somber lady in her mid-fifties with that same flaming hair as Sarah and her father. She introduced herself as Haddie Goodeign from Farmington, a small city two states over. She had arrived by train the night before and was surprised there wasn't any taxi service for visitors to get around. They told her it was a long story and that they needed to tell it to her as quickly as possible and that they really needed her cooperation. Miss Haddie, who had chosen not to Anglicize the old family surname, invited them to join her in the back apartment and have coffee, but they declined telling her it might be best to refrain from eating or drinking anything in the apartment or store.

The lady was two years older than Sarah's dad who was the youngest male of their generation. She frequently visited to run the store when the Goods went on vacation or took buying trips for the store. My dad asked her if she noticed anything out of order in any area of the store, basement or living quarters. Miss Haddie said her brother used the basement for overflow storage and that she had just found out about a safe down there when she spoke to the appraiser and that she hadn't been aware of it before.

She said the nice gentleman who had just left the store as they had come in referred to the safe when he

29

asked to see the three ancient volumes he'd come to appraise. Miss Haddie said she didn't believe they had much value because they were just musty and moldy to her, but that they had seemed to light a fire under him. She thought they were too dirty to even touch.

The mention of mold immediately struck a chord with the infectious disease nurse that had accompanied the officers. She asked if she could look at the volumes. Miss Haddie led them to an elaborate display that Sarah had set up. Her niece was obviously so excited by her find that she had given the volumes a place of honor near the counter on a raised podium, only there were only two and Miss Haddie had said the man had come to appraise three volumes. "Oh," she said when asked about the missing one, "the book appraiser took the first volume to start his research. He's got a camper at the Deer Lake Travel Park. He said all of his research books and his computer were in his RV."

The task force members that had entered the book store had all put on dust masks; however one look at the ancient leather bound books sent a shudder through all of them. The impressed lettering appeared to have once been gold leaf, but was more of a Verde green and a musty grey by that time. Everyone was ordered out of the building and an emergency call went out for a full response Haz-Mat team to pick up the two volumes from the store and test whatever it was that was on them. They called for a quarantine of the store, also a complete abatement of the free standing building if harmful elements were found on the volumes.

They asked Miss Haddie to get her purse from the apartment because an ambulance was on the way to take her to a quarantine ward at Capitol General Hospital.

No one knew how much exposure it took to cause the contamination and she had arrived in town last night. Miss Haddie told them that letting the appraiser into the store was the first time she had been in it since the last time she "store-sat" for her brother thirteen months ago. She, also, said she had trouble sleeping most nights. Since it had taken her until 3am to find someone to give her a ride from the train station, she had made a pot of coffee and sat on the east facing porch to wait for the dawn.

Everyone prayed there was hope for this kind lady.

Sarah Good had discovered the basement safe after her parents' fatal accident and if the tests proved positive for harmful spores, it was hoped the search for the infection connection would be over.

Another part of the task force was dispatched to the travel park with a second Haz-Mat team. Miss Haddie had given them the appraiser's name.

The registration clerk searched her log for the book expert's name and campsite. He had driven in pulling an Airstream and was assigned to lot #53 toward the back west end of the park. He had been in possession of the first volume for only the last two hours, so perhaps there would be hope for him is what was on the minds of those heading toward his camp. After all, at that point, it was still speculation; tests hadn't begun on anything yet.

Everything was quiet around the RV. The officer-in-charge's knock was answered by a gentle, "I'll be right there. Did I forget to pick up my messages?" The door was opened by a white haired angelic faced sixty-something-year-old in a red open neck shirt, white cardigan with elbow patches, and navy blue pants. Shoes had been left by the door, navy socks were a match. The inside of the RV seemed to be as orderly and well-appointed as its owner.

31

Mr. Gendusa was asked to exit the camper by officers showing their credentials. He was immediately clothed in a Haz-Mat suit as he was explained the circumstances of his hasty removal. Being the good citizen that he was, the man complied without fuss. Another team from The Center for Disease Control arrived and began to wrap and pack the entire Airstream and load it on a flatbed tow truck and it was taken to a federal facility. They also took his pickup truck since that's what he drove back to his camp site in with the volume from the book store.

According to my dad, "the genie had left the bottle." The TV folks were arriving; the country had found out that something was happening in Carverland County. He said he was afraid the cork would never fit the neck of the bottle again. I wasn't sure what he meant by that either, but again I was positive it meant something bad.

By noon the next day Miss Haddie still showed no signs of infection, but nothing good was going on with Mr. Gendusa. By that time he had dark circles under his eyes, his beautiful white hair was falling out but what hadn't fallen out had grown at least three inches and turned a sickly greenish grey. His nose was running pus and the flesh under his fingernails had turned black.

As hard as this was to watch, it was also enlightening for the authorities. First it gave a time line for the first signs of infection and progression of the outbreak in an adult male with a weakened immune system from contact with the fungi to the full blown Zombi Flu stage. However, even though the patients were under observation and the medical staff seemed to be compiling information and getting the answers to many questions, the scientists were still waiting for test results on the volumes, the book store, the rear

32

apartment, the RV, and the pickup. The common area of concentration was still on the mold spores since they were found in all the areas of concern

So, while the task force medical personnel and CDC staff were being kept very busy with their work, the rest of the task force returned to the call room to go back over the forensic reports and statements from the relatives. Most of the family members were being counseled at various churches and doctors' offices. The IT guy had transposed all of the statements and uploaded them so that everyone in the room could study them at once. Some folks were making notes of their own in little spiral black notebooks.

The same thoughts seem to be on everyone's minds, the book store was the common denominator. The parents all said that the children were so excited about touching "the 'big ancient books' that were almost as old as the bible!"; Gramps had shopped there for Granda's surprise; the taxi driver's wife wrote that Roger was an avid reader between fares and purchased used paperbacks there, she found a receipt dated five days before her husband's outbreak; and Alice Morgan had been planning her group's monthly meeting around the store's latest best sellers list. Of course the week earlier the teachers and the aid were on the field trip with the 5th and 6th graders. All clues pointed in one direction. Also, there hadn't been anymore incidents since the building had been quarantined.

A bulletin had been inserted into the front page of the local newspaper and on the internet in order to reach out to regular customers of the store. Anyone who had shopped at "Reading for the Future Books & Periodicals" since the Goods' fatal crash was asked to stay-in-place and call the sheriff's office immediately. As it turned out, in respect for the family's sudden loss, no one had attempted to approach Sarah for business until they felt she could get a handle on the day-to-day operations of the place. Since the field trip had been on the schedule since the beginning of the school year, it had gone on as planned. Sarah and the teachers had not wanted to disappoint the children.

The forensic investigation of the book store records was conducted by three Haz-Mat clothed technicians who studied each page that had been carefully separated from log and ledger books and slipped into sealed plastic sleeves. Records of books received, books sold, and books in inventory were checked and cross checked. Receipts for the mortgage payoff, building maintenance, utilities and office supplies were reviewed. One order for work performed to install a basement safe was dated eleven years ago after a special shipment had been delivered in protective packaging and post marked by the postal service to be from the Channel Islands off the California Coast, per a hand written note.

There wasn't anything in the notes about who sent the package or what it contained, only that the safe was installed to contain it. And that was something that intrigued my dad. The note said the safe was to "contain" the package until after 2000, not "for the contents" of the package until after 2000. There was nothing mentioned about the package being opened. What was it that the Goods' knew needed to be contained without looking inside?

My dad said it felt like the world was in suspended animation while everyone waited for the scientists' reports.

It was decided that Miss Haddie would most likely be released soon and allowed to go back to her home, but never again to the store and she was only told that mold spores had invaded the store because of a flood that had happened in the basement before Sarah moved to town. She was also told that her niece had had a fatal anaphylactic shock reaction to that mold. In fact, the task force legal staff had written up an order of imminent domain to be signed by a local judge and presented to the family's attorney in order that the building and its basement could be brought down by a county Haz-Mat work crew. Fr. Dean was busy readying a huge quantity of Holy Water.

Mr. Gendusa was not as fortunate. In his quarantine room he had continued to spiral down into the agony, rage, and filth of the Zombi Flu symptoms. His skin became pocked, blistered and bruised, his hair matted with ooze, and the odor in the room rose to a level that permeated the glass enclosure which caused a sense of fear for contamination. What if this flu had been air born like some other viruses were? And another question began to arise for the task force, would it be legal to "put Mr. Gendusa down" in a situation like they had? Could the county claim self-defense? The leather restraints were weakening, the howls were getting worse, and the degree of rage was unimaginable in this previously gentle, cooperative man.

The lab reports began to come in. As expected, the greenish dust tinting the embossed lettering on the old volumes was a type of mold. But the genome of this organism contained elements of at least five various mold spores not known to current man and science. The carbon dating of the leather binding tested out to be at least as old as the 1940's and the leather itself proved to be tanned and processed human skin. Under the mold the embossed letters were indeed expensive gold leaf.

Swabs from Mr. Gendusa's nostrils while he was sedated in the early stages of his decline were full of the same mold spores. There were also spores taken from biopsies of his lungs, but unlike the dry spores of his nose, the wet spores in his lungs showed no sign of life.

The tests also showed that the mold attached itself only to items that came in direct contact with it. The spores proved to have tiny cilia that gave them a crawling motion but did not give them flight and that they were very top heavy. The transference from the books to Mr. Gendusa's nostrils were obviously completed by hand-to-face contact.

To the relief of those working the quarantine room, it was determined that the virus traveled by direct contact rather than by air. Everyone affected by the Zombi Flu had handled the volumes then physically touched their victims who then showed signs of infection if not killed by their raging attackers.

With all of the measures that had been put in place, it seemed that the end of the crisis may have been in sight. The spread looked like it was at an end. And since science had identified the cause to be a virus, Holy Water was no longer needed, but still couldn't hurt and every church's prayers were still being said for the county.

The issue of the legality of Mr. Gendusa's fate settled itself. He broke free of his restraints and, with extraordinary strength, hurled a metal institutional side table at the glass wall and totally shattered it. The two military guards on duty both emptied their 45 Cal Desert Eagles into his head and torso, more out of surprise than heroism, but it still did the job. Even though the cause of the outbreak was scientifically explainable, the stricken were still hard to kill and physical contact was definitely out of the question.

When symptoms started to show, Mr. Gendusa's brother had been informed over the phone that he had taken very ill with a sudden heart attack and that it had sent him and his camping outfit careening into an old live oak and killed him instantly. He wasn't from a well off family and according to his brother had very little insurance. The undertaker who called offered an outstanding cremation and shipping arrangement that the family couldn't help but accept. Of course nothing of Mr. Gendusa would actually be in the sealed attractive urn provided by the "Carverland County Indigent Visitors' Burial Program", a term that had been concocted by the city manager's secretary. This was the same benefit that was afforded to Miss Haddie and her family with Sarah's remains. In actuality, Mr. Gendusa's ashes had followed Sarah's ashes down St. Monica's sacristy drain.

It still wasn't known who or why the Goods had been mailed the package of three contaminated volumes eleven years ago but there wasn't any evidence of any other such packages coming to the little store or anywhere else in our county. And we'd never know why the book store owners never unveiled the contents of the basement safe that Sarah felt was so astounding and whether they were keeping the volumes or the town safe all these years or just waiting for the right time to expose them to the town.

Everyone was really tired and I had fallen asleep in my dad's squad car, again, but another meeting was called. All of the questions had been answered; all of the dangers of the spores had been secured. It did seem like everything was winding down. There wasn't any more danger in the town; there hadn't been any outbreaks in four days which was determined to be thirty-six hours beyond the virus' incubation period. However, the powers-that-be decided to test everyone's anxiety a bit longer and waited another five days to make sure everyone's stories matched up. Now damage control was more important than anything else and had to be put in place properly.

A press conference was called on Monday morning by The State Police Commander, who stood at the podium and was joined by the Chatawa Mayor, Carverland Sheriff, Yotashi Fire Chief, District Attorney Harper, and Major Howard from the "Wild Bears" National Guard Artillery Unit, all strategically positioned on the stage behind him. All of the officials were in their respective uniforms, medals, and name badges. They were quite an intimidating sight with no question as to authority. Deliberately absent from the group was anybody representing the CDC so as not to arouse any unwanted suspicion about the story they were about to tell.

None of the town's civilian population was in attendance either. They had been through enough and did not need the added attention of the paparazzi.

The media was ushered into the City Hall cafeteria where the conference was scheduled. There wasn't that many people in attendance because secrecy about the county's horrible events had been considerably successful. The mid-west county was small and most people knew or were related to everyone else. Neighbors and neighborhoods were important to everybody and they didn't want to be ostracized by the rest of their state or the rest of the country. The Genie was kept in the bottle after all.

So a sequence of unrelated and regrettable tragedies were listed and explained in perfectly typed sheets that were handed out to thoroughly account for the news reports of the last four weeks.

The State Commander began by addressing the attendees this way, "Ladies and Gentlemen, first of all I and my comrades would like to thank you for your time and patience. I know some of you have heard murmurs or rumors of odd happenings around the county. In actuality, it's all been a series of illnesses and tragic accidents that fell together in an unexpected manner."

Then he proceeded to recount everything on the typed sheets about heart attacks, disorientation, anaphylactic shock, traffic accidents, and most heart rending of all to explain, the propane tank explosion at the school bus barn.

Then in closing the Commander said, "So I'm sure you'll understand if we as a community ask you as charitable, understanding American citizens, to leave us to mourn and absorb our losses. Thank you."

Then he and the others turned to walk away feeling like they had successfully put everything to rest.

But just then a tall gentleman with curly red hair and a cargo vest with a 35mm camera hanging from his neck stood up and waved his hand. "Excuse me, Sir," he called out, "but could your 'sequence of unrelated and regrettable tragedies' have anything to do with the same kind of 'unrelated and regrettable tragedies' reported this week that has come out of that township in Canada?"

No one really took notice that he spoke with a European accent.

CHANUCK'S WILDERNESS LIFE

He loved the air this time of year and loved the turning of the landscape. At a time when others hibernated, he elected life in the outdoors. He loved it when the cold air ripped into his lungs and challenged him to keep breathing. He lived to run long and leap high, to howl with the wolf and sight with the eagle. And the animals knew him, tolerated him, feared him, and respected him because he could be their friend, their foe, or their worst enemy. He could protect them, but if they crossed the wrong path into his territory, he would hunt them and because there was mostly man inside his blood, when they got caught, they got caught badly.

He had lived here for the last eleven years when it became obvious to him that it was safer for himself and his family that he leave the city and find a place to live alone. And of course "alone" was relevant to the attitude with which you chose to approach life. Some beasts lived with him and some beasts couldn't.

He hadn't known what his grandfather was hinting to when he said there was a secret he had to share with him in the barn. Popy was the youngest son of the Wanaka Way pet shop owners who were from "the old country", but Chanuck didn't know he still had anything from "the old country" with him in this wonderful country in which they lived. Popy had always said that coming here after those terrible times of hiding and fighting and being hungry all the time was the best thing his father had done for our family. He'd said that if

41

the family had started back there, his grandson would not have had the good blood that he did have today.

But that good blood had proven to be a matter of opinion. Maybe a better description for the blood was engineered.

Popy showed him a set of very old books that seemed to be a sort of log of someone's life. The books were extremely old and he was told they were bound from very expensive leather. They were labeled in brilliant gold letters.

The labeling read, "The Past and Future of the Family's Line, Volume A". There were three of them titled in the same manner with the exceptions of "Volume B" and "Volume C" changes. They were the finest books he had ever seen in his twenty-two years and they had all been written by somebody identified only as "Eric".

His grandfather assigned him one week to complete the task of reading each of the large volumes from beginning to end without any questions asked until the last page was done. The old man's days had been ending soon and the family's lineage and purpose needed to be handed down to his youngest male heir. And fortunately or unfortunately this fell to Chanuck.

Popy was an avid hunter, but he had never asked to join him on any of those many trips. It had been on one of these four night forays into the high country that his dad had been lost when Chanuck was still a baby. Popy had returned with deep scratches and gouges laden with rock chips and dust from the granite formations for which the Canadian wilderness was known. He said that his youngest son had slipped into a deep crevice and that he too had almost lost his life in an attempt to pull him back to safety but lost his grip in the end. He even said his son's cries could be heard for a full minute before he finally hit the bottom and heard the cries abruptly stop.

The story had continued that his grandfather had camped by the site for another twenty-four hours in hope of hearing some sign of life. He said he had also dropped a flare into the crevice to no avail.

A memorial service had been held and Popy continued his patriarchal leadership of the family. Mormy had given Popy two daughters who, with their husbands from "new country" bloodlines, had in turn given him two grandchildren each. However, his youngest child and only son had only blessed him with one grandson at the time of his demise. Eleven years ago, that grandson had been informed of the cursed torch he must carry.

WILD INSTINCTS

It was difficult to understand. He'd never acted out like this before and one eye was completely dangling from its socket. But the rat was worst of all. Its body looked to have been totally obliterated. If I hadn't seen the rat before the Chihuahua Mix got a hold of it, I wouldn't have been able to tell what animal it had been, other than mammal.

But why had this happened? The little dog had gone into the forest last night and wouldn't return when it was called. The rat always hung around the storage shed. It was probably a pet that had been set loose. Its white on brown coat was more typical of a pet bred critter than a city pest. Now neither animal was what it had been just twenty-four hours ago.

My dad was the oldest veterinarian in our small town and one of only four in the province. A lot of his territory encompassed wilderness areas. Sometimes his patients included beaver or muskrat or owls and not all of them were wild. Up here many folks turned to unconventional pets for companionship. Some of the weather where humans lived this far north was a bit too harsh for the average cat or dog or parakeet. And some of the unconventional got into unimaginable problems living in man's world.

This was something else though and nothing had ever been average about this animal. First of all, this little dog had been born out in the barn during the middle of a harsh winter. Fortunately for him, he was an only pup and his long coated mother gave him all of her body heat, attention and warm milk he needed to survive. The smart instinctive little bitch used a critter's nest she discovered in the bottom of a hay bin for a whelping box and that helped her to comfortably incubate her suckling.

When spring came and the snow melted, we found them both barking for attention on the front porch. My dad figured she'd kept them both going by feeding off of mice and blue moles because that summer brought on a pests free season in the out buildings.

The two small dogs stayed on the homestead with us so we just named them Mother and Son. We thankfully thought little of the fact that we were never infested by rodents during the next three years.

When Mother had showed up with her new little pup, my dad could tell she was about seven years old and figured that the reason she had only one pup in her litter. They were both in good health so Dad gave each one the shots needed to protect them against any and all known canine health threats for the area and neutered them both.

We had other dogs on the property more apt to cold weather, but no one ever remembered seeing the two share bed with the others or eat from any of the food pans, still they stayed healthy and fit. But one day something strange took place that no one would ever be able to forget.

Son had seemed to be avoiding Mother for the last few days. She had been growling and snorting and snapping at everything and everyone, him included. We were sitting out on the porch that night, the moon was full and high in the sky, and stars could be seen for what looked like eternity in the distance. There was the sounds of her snarls and rage coming from under the pump shed but we had sort of gotten used to her angry attitude for the last three or four days. Mother was so mean at this point that Daddy couldn't even examine her to see if she was hurt and if pain was the reason for her awful change in attitude.

Snowshoe, the long, lean Siamese mix with the four white boots was crossing the front yard. He was a rather big boned cat who had come to us after at least five seasons of feral breeding. Unlike most males who are neutered as kittens, Snowshoe had a big head and strong muscular front legs, shoulders, and hind quarters from years of fighting other inner city street cats for the right to mate stray females. He had taken to neuter life well, but still commanded respect among our other cats and huskies alike.

All of a sudden, Mother came charging out from under the pump house and ran right up to Snowshoe, grabbing him violently by the side of his belly and shaking him in her mouth left to right over and over again and slamming him repeatedly into the ground. It all happened so suddenly and violently that no living creature in sight of the carnage could move for the sheer shock of it all.

Mother was not a large canine, standing no more than nine inches at the crown of her head, yet she held the eleven pound male cat firmly in her jaws in the air over her head and continued to swing him from side to side. Snowshoe yowled and hissed and clawed the air in vain. Blood was being flung all over both of them and all over the dirt yard. The other dogs began to bark and seemed to think they could come to the cat's aid. Dad had been cleaning cages in the kennel rooms of his clinic and came running out of the back door with an over and under in his two hands. But even he was stopped in his tracks.

It wasn't a wild animal like a coyote or a bear harming his "pack", but an eight pound mix breed terrier, horribly living up to the origin of its breed genus.

Snowshoe was showing the effects of the vicious attack. His head and limbs and even his tail were flailing lifelessly as he was buffeted from side to side. My dad walked up to the scene with the shotgun trained on the small female dog. With the most chilling look of understanding and defiance, Mother slowly placed the lifeless body of the cat on the ground, stared my dad in the eyes and high-tailed it into the woods. In unison the husky pack raised their heads and let out the most mournful howl, and then the yard immediately went totally silent as if in instant mourning for the family's loss.

My mom tapped me on the leg and slowly pointed at the small figure lying with his chin resting on his front paws. There was Son as relaxed as if about to dream about a fun day running in clover. He had watched his mother's attack and the death of his yard-mate without any emotion at all, not a bark, not even an attempted howl. It was almost as if he had viewed it all in a fugue. Yet, every other creature, human or fur person alike had eyes of tears and dismay.

Dad shooed the other animals away from the grisly scene and had all of us go inside. Mom tried to change the attitude in the air by offering hot chocolate with marshmallows and whipped cream. We halfheartedly began getting out our mugs and sitting around the kitchen table. We heard the pump kick on and the water start beating against the ground as Daddy began cleaning away the proof of what we'd just witnessed. Lonnie was first, then Jeff, Mom was at the sink with her head bowed, then I couldn't hold back any longer. It was a wonder the room didn't flood from the tears.

The hot chocolate had done nothing for my mood and I needed to find out what had caused the slaughter that resulted from a previously quiet, loving little creature turning into a wild flesh rendering mauler.

Without my folks knowing, I tried to follow Mother's trail into the wilderness. Being a small dog, she didn't exactly cut a path into the bush, but she did leave a trail of blood along the lower branches of scrub. She was freshly covered in Snowshoe's splatters. I didn't have very far to go, though. Mother traveled about a quarter of a mile into the forest, then tumbled head over heels, as if her front half had stopped and didn't know her back half was still coming. She laid there still as a rock, the birds and insects grew ominously quiet.

Then I heard twigs cracking under something's weight. I wasn't going to be there alone for long and hid behind a thick holly growing in the center of three trees.

A tall well-muscled man with long striking red hair streaked with blond bands of color and tied with a red handkerchief walked over to the small body. He wore denims, hiking boots and an unbuttoned blue flannel shirt with rolled up sleeves. The hair on his arms and chest seemed dusted with a fine grey powder. His body language said he was very sad as he picked up the lifeless dog, cradling her as he walked back the same way he'd come.

I felt something wasn't right here and headed back home not knowing how I'd report this to my dad without revealing my own behavior sneaking off the property. However, I knew my folks would want to be told about a stranger wandering about the forest at night less than a mile from our homestead.

The pet store on Wanaka Way was opened in 1954 by a couple who migrated to the province from Nova Scotia. They had two olive complected sons with deep auburn hair and the sons honored them with two grandsons. The sons had married girls of Scandinavian

49

decent and their sons were born with beautiful green or grey eyes and heads full of light auburn hair. They were handsome descendants that any grand-folks would have been proud of but worry was all you ever saw in the old people's eyes.

Eleven years ago, the old Romanian couple passed their shop on to their oldest son, Jameil. He moved his family into the old living quarters at the rear of the business and added on an upper level with additional bedrooms to accommodate his larger brood of two sons, Jovian and Juvenal and a daughter, Juanea. The girl married her high school sweetheart and followed him to Calgary for work.

The oldest son, Jovian, had chosen a career in the Royal Canadian Mounted Police and loved the typical outdoor life. He housed his family in a large log cabin at the edge of town. He put in long hours on the job and didn't want a long commute. His wife always said his spirit was as wild as the world he worked in.

The younger, Juvenal, on the other hand continued running the pet store after their parents retired. He seemed to literally speak to the animals that passed through the store. He always had a calming effect on new animals until they adjusted to the stares and voices of the curious customers and their excited children. His wife would take on running the store while Juvenal spent time in the storeroom with new arrivals. By the time they were brought out to be exhibited, even the reptiles were as calm as hand raised puppies. He seemed to exude a peace to the animals in stark contrast to their cousin Chanuck.

The brothers were as different as day and night. Yet they had in common obvious things: they both loved to work at night and both brothers' skin tended to cover over with a grey dust the way other humans' skin covered with sweat. Juvenal experienced much less of this oddity than his brother, but still had a shower stall in the storeroom downstairs behind the pet store and always came "home" upstairs smelling fresh and clean no matter how long he'd spent in the store room with the animals. Jovian, however, had to have all his uniforms, even shirts, dry cleaned weekly because of the grey dust that always formed on the inside of them and just caked up when washed the conventional way. These weren't things that the general public knew, but that would come to the forefront eventually.

Some of the campers were sleeping peacefully in pop-up pull behinds. It was nearly three AM in the night and the moon was full and high giving plenty of light for wild eyes to see. They didn't really need light because they were given great sight by Nature to hunt at night when it was safer for them. They could come out during day, if food was scarce, but this site promised to supply them with enough food to cache away for the spring months as well. This was an important hunt and they had sent out yowls that invited other lairs to join them also, since they were small and the prey was large and many.

The rest of the "food" source was in many individual rounded covers, but the materials were lite and yielded easily to sharp claws that were always kept on the ready from climbing on ruff bark and hard stone. They didn't usually feel this bold in spite of their wild instincts, but the wonderful spores they detected coming off of the shirtless male human had filled them with great excitement and courage. And their senses seemed to be intoned to one mind.

As one body, short bob tails straight out, the leader of each den reached forward and ripped the tent and canvas walls from top to bottom. Thoughts were easily heard in the minds of each animal, yet the night stayed eerily quiet to those sleeping inside. Each member entered on silent pads and stealthily positioned themselves over the sleeping food. Even they were perplexed by the change in their thinking. It was almost as if they thought like the human from whom they had gotten the spores.

The leaders let out a guttural snarl that signaled the attack as it also awakened the prey and the carnage began. At first the wrappings the food was in posed a barrier to their goal, but the frantic struggles of the humans to escape the pack actually loosened them from the wrappings and exposed them to the sharp, rendering claws and gripping jaws. Though they weren't very large, each of the pack members had the savage strength they needed to carry away the prizes by the throat. By the time they reached their dens, the prey had mostly bled out and the major struggle was over.

The feasting began as each pack member settled in a separate space where it could sup in peace. The female which had remained in the den with her kits because they were too young to leave alone, stood and licked her lips as her mate brought her a very small prey that he laid at her paws. He walked over to a much lesser pack member and stole the majority of its meal. As their bellies got full, each animal moved to a special spot and began burying the remains of their feast for leaner times as the still cold season passed on. The effects of the spores were fading as the felines settled down for their day time sleep.

They had no idea about the severity of the night's hunt and the human wrath that would come down on their dens as a consequence to their actions. Their enhanced instinct to prepare for the upcoming solstice only sparked the need to stock the dens. Having no sense of future or consequence beyond preparing for winter food shortages, the wild creatures had no idea what would happen when man found out about the loss of an entire camp of his kind.

The only blood found in the remains of the tents proved to be human and all of the tracks found on the ground were small cat prints. There wasn't any sign of rabies in the fluids found on the victims' clothing, but a grey spore found on the bedding in the tents was sent to a lab in Toronto for analysis. There were eighteen lives taken that night and no one had ever given any thought as to how many bobcats called the territory home, but it was certain that they all had to die now.

Civilized man had shared this wilderness with the fauna since the continent was discovered without such a decimated camp report as this one. Big Game Hunters were called in to aid the Mounties in their quest to make the region safe.

Though evidence revealed less than twenty animals were in the camp, the experienced hunters hired by the town brought down more than thirty cats in their relentless effort to earn as much bounty as possible from the Province. Camping and fishing clubs provided a large part of the civic earnings and tragedies like what had occurred that week could drastically reduce those earnings and raise taxes on every resident.

The old bob-tom lay up on the boulder in the warm sun and took his regular afternoon nap. The farmer had watched him through his field sites for over three years and never felt any danger from the old boy nearly a mile away. And the big cat had never caused any need for danger alarm to his livestock or his family and the animal felt just as safe going through its daily routine. But today the farmer didn't just site him through his scope to admire the tom's prowess, today he took

53

careful aim and fired his Winchester 70 with lightning speed. The animal's body jumped from the impact of the 300 Mag bullet before the roar of the gun's explosion left the farmer's ear and was thrown from its favored rock.

The farmer sent one of his hands out to retrieve the lifeless body. The man put the corpse in an old feed sack and threw it in the back of his boss' pickup. The old tom was not shown any of the dignity with which he had once ruled his den.

The farmer left immediately for my father's clinic on the other edge of town to find out just how close a danger the mature male bobcat had presented.

My dad hadn't been involved in what the big game hunters were doing out in the forest. They only had to bring in the tails to prove and collect on their kills. Daddy made sure the family pets were all penned so no hunting mistakes could occur.

Son had disappeared from the property soon after the camp sight event. He had chewed his way out of his hard wood and chicken wire pen which had been enough restraint for him for the last three years until now. He had changed a lot since Mother's horrific behavior and disappearance. No one saw him go, but the damage to his pen was horrendous and all indications were of a break out not a break in. The little fellow had left on his own. The only hint of what had prompted his run was the similarity of his attack on the rat to Mother's attack on Snowshoe and the way she had left after.

When Mr. Dureaux showed up with the old tom's caucus, my dad was puzzled as to just what he wanted. A forensic exam on a deceased human is an autopsy and on an animal it's called a necropsy, that's what the farmer wanted Dad to perform on the wild feline. His farm was ten miles out from where the event took place and he wanted to know if he should talk to the hunters about hunting over in his area, too.

The results of the necropsy drew mixed emotions. Not only were Old Bob Tom's systems lacking any signs of human ingestion, but the corpse showed none of the spores left at the killing scene or on the animals' tails the hunters had brought in. The whole thing left Mr. Dureaux with some feelings of regret.

I thought it was time I confessed and told my dad about my trip into the woods behind Mother. Things were moving so fast in so many directions, I thought I should add what I witnessed into the mix. I told him about following Son's mom for nearly half a mile before she collapsed. Then I told him about the tall man with the fuzzy looking stuff all over the hairs on his chest and arms and about how he lovingly carried the dead dog in his arms. Daddy was immediately on his feet and holding me firmly by both arms. I knew I was in so much trouble then, but instead of going into a tirade about my misbehavior, my dad began a ton of questions about the stranger.

I gave him the best description I could about the man and his clothes. He, also, wanted me to take him and the constable and his deputies down the exact trail I'd taken. I didn't know it until then, but the results had come back on the analysis of the spores from the tents. He called the hospital and requested a Haz Mat team, too.

By the time the Mounties arrived, my dad and the Haz Mat case leader were informing everyone on the results of the lab tests and the fact that scientists from the Center for Disease Control in Atlanta, Georgia were making their way to our area of the hemisphere.

55

The spores found at our scene were of the same phyla but different genus of those found in the American Mid-West. The spores found in that county wide case had resulted in the mental and physical degradation that evolved into a Lethal DNA. There hadn't been any reports of human attackers in this region yet, but with the changes in the behavior of Son and Mother and the never before heard of communal cooperation among the bobcat dens to attack mankind, the doctors were afraid the spores were mutating. One thing was confusing though, it seemed the spores in one location were affecting people and the spores in the other location were affecting animals, but why not both in either location. All of the infected were warm blooded, all were in good health by all indication and only one had a weakened immune system. The blood and cells in the tails of the hunted bobcats tested out as having belonged to healthy felines and the available medical records of the mid-westerners showed generally healthy individuals as well.

The official report going out to the press and families about the camp site massacre was a plague outbreak. It had been carried by vermin that nested in the wheel wells of planes flying overhead from the Desert Southwest U.S. and had fallen out as they flew over the area. Relatives were told that due to the highly contagious nature of the infection and flea infestation introduced into the area by the animals, all of the victims were cremated and returned to the families in impressive urns at the Provence's expense.

It was that explanation and solution that had some media starting to connect the dots.

The second lieutenant in charge of the Mounty troop assigned to the case explained that their commander had a sudden emergency and might be able to meet them along the trail later but they were in radio communication with him. The commander had family in the area and would contact them as soon as he'd spoken with his brother, however they hadn't heard back from him yet.

Juvenal was surprised when his brother called with news of the forces coming into the forest and that the authorities knew about the spores. The brothers heard about the failure of the project in the mid-west, but Jovian was determined to fulfill their family's part of the mission. Canada needed to feel the outrage of their tribe so they knew they had to warn their cousin Chanuck.

There was still the plan that was being carried out in the South as well and that would still touch America on an even wider scale. There was still third generation hope.

If the cousins in the mid-west had followed the instructions that they got after their grandfather's death eleven years ago, instead of hiding the magnificent spores in what amounted to "an unmarked grave", this whole process would have been on track. They and their cousins were the grand and great grandchildren of the famous triplets who had left Romania as little more than teenagers themselves in order to honor and revenge the brave martyrs of their tortured village. The brothers carried a huge amount of dedication in their hearts.

After losing his son, Popy wanted to be sure the capsules he'd protected for so many years didn't bring harm to his youngest grandson and only chance of carrying on the family's Swovatnian name. He wanted to make sure the spores were indeed harmless to his family if taken internally since that was the only way they could metabolize into the weapon his grandson would be commissioned to release. So, before his son was conceived, Popy swallowed two of the eight capsules in the cherished bottle handed down to him by his father.

For the next year, Popy felt anxious about his bold move, but nothing threatening happened to his health. At the same time he had invited his brother over for coffee and secretly dropped two capsules 'into his mug.

When his nephews Jovian and Juvenal were born, Popy watched their development closely, noticing their interaction with animals and the grey powdery effect on their body hair which the pediatrician could not explain. Still they grew strong and healthy in spite of carrying their father's metabolic adjustment. By the time they were four and Chanuck was five, Popy was sure the capsules would perform their promised tasks without harm.

Just before he entered puberty, Popy gave Chanuck the four remaining spore pods to swallow. Being aware of the family lure, the boy did as he was told.

Popy had watched with great concern as the pre-teen rapidly developed prowess and instinct during the hormonal explosion that happens as child blossoms into teenager into young adult.

Chanuck spent more and more time in the forest and less time at home with him and Mormy. When he wanted to live on his own, he moved into a cottage deep in the woods.

With another curious explanation for an unnatural amount of unlikely deaths, it was evident to the brothers that their cousin was performing his part in the plan on schedule. However, the blundering by the mid-west tribe had greatly threatened the entire plan.

Jovian and Juvenal were determined to help Chanuck see their ancestors' plans through.

It was easy to find their cousin even though his house was locked up tight. To the brothers, Chanuck's trail of grey spores was as evident as Hansel's and Gretel's bread crumbs. So the two traveled deeper into the forest and noticed the animal carnage increase as they went. This affected Juvenal more since he maintained such a peaceful rapport with animals he reached out to. Jovian, on the other hand usually used his ability to ward off animal contact.

There were a few areas where the earth was disturbed and they could tell these were resting places that had been shallowly dug out and covered with great remorse. One of the graves was that of a rather small female dog which had died with her eyes staring straight ahead as if in terror. Juvenal empathized with her pain.

Eventually they happened upon what appeared to be a nest in the bough of a huge fir that had been obviously struck by lightning and split early in its growth to create such a large resting place. It was a very large nest and it was covered with grey dust, or as they knew, grey spores.

The nest began to rustle and become unsettled; the brothers each put their hands to the sidearm that was holstered at their sides. Jovian had shed his Mounty uniform and both brothers looked like your typical woodsmen out for a few rabbits to bring home for a good stew. Only they knew they were far from that.

Being so isolated, it was quite obvious that Chanuck would know little of the horde that was about to descend on him and his domain. The brothers began to call out his name and yell out who they were as well. "Chanuck, Chanuck, cousin its Jovian and Juvenal, Bro", yelled one. "We've come to help you out, Cuz" called out the other.

The nest grew still, the air was eerily quiet, nothing moved, even the wind was gone. Then they heard, "I'm inside and I'm coming out, but you've got to know I'm naked. Don't freak out". A thin wall on the left side of the nest shook and they saw a grey dusty arm emerge with long stiff hairs on the underside, then a shoulder, leg and finally a head with the rest of Chanuck following. The hair on his chest and thighs was no longer than usual, but the hair on his back, buttocks and underside of his arms was as long and stiff as the four inch red locks on his head. And Chanuck and the nest smelled like wet towels left in the bottom of a clothes hamper for a week in the middle of summer. It was no wonder he was nude, clothes would have been quite uncomfortable. Their cousin's face, however, was as clean and smooth as when they were all boys.

"Chanuck, what's happened here, what is that you were in? It looks like some sort of nest!" was what Juvenal blurted out first.

"We're here to help you man, my whole Mounty troop is on the way to your forest. They know about the spores. They are afraid of something like what took place in the U.S. Mid-West happening here. And man, some kid saw you pick up their little dog that went crazy when it died."

Their cousin's eyes seemed to have hazed over, it was doubtful he could see at all and it was then that they noticed movements in the hairs. But a second look proved the movements were from the hairs themselves. Much like a cat's whiskers, the hairs seemed to detect Chanuck's proximity to people or objects and service him in the absence of eyesight.

He affirmed their suspicions. Ever since the spore dust had covered his eyes, Chanuck had been able to sense items and movement through the sensors on the hair tips and that enabled him to move around his world with confidence.

The constant movement of the hairs though was eerie.

He, also, confirmed that the small dog the brothers had unearthed was in deed one of his first experiments that resulted to his satisfaction, though he regretted the death of the little dog he'd watched raise her male pup so lovingly and then her grown pup, as well.

His second great success was the attack by the bobcats; however he lived with even greater regret over that effort. Though the animals had responded to his emotional, mental commands, Chanuck had under estimated the brutal organized response that the authorities of the Province would inflict on the perpetrators. He knew he had to gain more control and build up enough spore product to affect more animals at one time to conduct an all-out major surprise attack with no chance of reprise. That was the purpose of the nest.

Jovian and Juvenal got a pang of apprehension at the same time and maybe it was just brought on by Chanuck's unusual appearance. However, there was also something odd about his voice and his movements. It wasn't just the weird constant movement of the hairs, but there was also a jerky spasm about the way his head kept going from left to right or up and down as if someone or something was moving him like a puppet on strings. What was wrong with him?

As the wind blew the nest from side to side, they noticed a sort of dust rise out of the branches and leaves that comprised most of the material of the structure. It looked almost as thick as clouds coming from a pit smoker and they started to wonder if something had happened to Chanuck while he sat in the nest breathing in the dust.

The spores had been engineered to be metabolized into the circulatory system of the body and exuded through the pores of the skin. They would then be expelled into the air and taken into the respiratory systems of other mammals targeted by Chanuck. That with his inherent ability to commune with them and the knowledge of the torch that he must carry and the legacy he had to fulfill, would set the animals on an unquenchable thirst for blood and an appetite for human flesh that would turn the pristine Canadian mountainside ruby red and ravaged.

The attack of the bobcats on the camp site had gone just as Chanuck had intended while he was in a perfect state of mind. His only error was in not being aware of the general state of mind of the northern hemisphere after the suspicious lost-of-life reports coming out of the mid-west. He lived more in the forest then in the civilized world, out of the general population and with little news from the outside world.

By all indications, he had enough spore build up to enact a large scale attack, but if his mind was off, the whole project was well in jeopardy. The procedure was based on the spore ejection eroding the other mammals' mental stability, but Chanuck was mammal too and he'd definitely been breathing the spores. That had to have been what the cloud coming out of the nest was made from.

If the project in the mid-west had gone off as planned and this project would unfold correctly the next step would be for the family branch on the Southern East Coast of the U.S. to "pull-the-lineal-trigger". But it hadn't gone right and now Chanuck's role in the tribe's retribution was more important than ever and no one could be allowed to fail it or expose the village's involvement in the plot, not even their loved and revered cousin.

Of course the boys had never traveled to Europe to visit the homeland of the family's "old country" roots. They had no idea that the tribe was long since dispersed and the village was turned into a city's subdivision.

They had been keeping up with the Southern tribe through Facebook so they were aware that their distant cousin Ivan was in prison and couldn't imagine how he would fulfill his destiny on time or at any time. So to them, their situation and need to succeed was critical.

They watched their branch's leader of the tribe's hope stumbling around jerkily and mumbling about small dogs and bobcats.

It was then that the two young men noticed a strange look in the blinded eyes of Chanuck, almost as if seeing something only their owner could perceive, with wet red tears streaming from them. Was he hearing his own crazed mental instructions to search and destroy mankind?

Chanuck needed watching for more reasons than one. If he was to succeed, he needed to be protected from the Mounted Police Officers that were quickly approaching. The project needed to be protected from Chanuck running amuck and making the authorities aware of the impending danger. The elements of surprise and confusion were important weapons in the plan.

While their cousin kept mumbling and stumbling, yet never running into anything because of those twitching grey hairs, the brothers began to hash out a plan. They felt like the family's legacy was in their hands. After all they also had mutated and enhanced metabolisms and were of the same ancient bloodline.

They also knew they had to act fast.

"I've got grey spore hair, man. It gets all over my uniform every day", said Jovian, "and you know you can get most animals to do whatever you want." Juvenal knew he was right, but wondered just where his brother was going with it.

"What are you saying? You never mentioned it being anything but a nuisance before."

"Yeah, well I never thought of having to depend on it for anything before."

"Well, how do you mean to depend on it now?" Juvenal wanted to know.

Jovian's thoughts went to what was needed to be done and what they had to work with. He had never tried to influence any other living being with his dusty skin condition, but desperation was affecting his emotions.

He knew how Juvenal could calm the pet shop animals to put up with any stress the shoppers and rowdy children could dish out. If his dust could get the animals' attention and his brother's telepathy could direct their emotions and actions, the ancestors' plans might still be salvaged in spite of Chanuck's apparent breakdown.

The brothers coaxed Chanuck back into the nest and helped him seal up the opening. They didn't see where any worse damage could be done to him among the spore dust than had already occurred. They headed back to his cabin to work out their own plan for success of the tribe's revenge. They felt part of their clan had been forced to live outside of their Romanian homeland by what this country's soldiers had rained on their people, so the duty to carry out the revenge was as much theirs as their cousin's. The tribe's wishes would still be fulfilled.

The Mounties, the Constable's officers, the scientists from the CDC, the HazMat unit and my dad entered the forest from the east. I had wanted to go along but my dad wouldn't budge on his commitment to keep my mom and us safely shuttered back at our cabin. After giving him exact directions to the spot where I had seen Mother drop and the dusty man take her body, I was sternly turned back home.

The disturbed grave of the little dog which had gone mad was discovered by the advancing men and women. A few feet away a cadaver dog alerted on another site. They uncovered the stiff body and staring eyes of Son. One of the scientists remarked that a full bobcat corpse that had been brought in by the hunters revealed the same unseeing stare. There was obviously a connection not only from the out of ordinary actions of the animals but from their physical appearance as well.

The canines had died practically while still in the throes of their madness. The felines had returned to their dens and appeared to settle back into the routine of life caching away the remnants of the kill. However, the hunters had acknowledged that the cats were exceptionally easy to come up on and slaughter. They were larger than the small dogs, so dying from the spore infection may have been taking longer to result.

The process of respiratory infection had been determined by the necropsy of the hunter's specimen and the on sight evidence of grey spore dust around the muzzles of Mother and Son. What they hadn't determined was the source of the spores. The scientists were, however, able to determine that the U. S. Mid-West spores and the Canadian spores were related even though the method of infection from each differed. One entered the victim's body through the skin and the other entered through the nostrils and both were definitely engineered, not natural. The other mystery surrounding the spores was that never before had any biological relative of these fungi ever been reported anywhere in the world before. The CDC was imbedded in laboratories around the world and the world knew nothing about them.

The two things that had been determined so far from the two events was that the spores and their spread was cancelled out by fire and though the Mid-West spores lived on after the death of their hosts unless set afire, the Canadian spores died once the infected host died. However, the trail way spores found along plant leaves and vines in the vicinities of the infected animals lived without the aid of a host and did not penetrate the plant. It was assumed that if additional animals came along and sniffed those plants and vines, the madness would have spread. All of the posse members wore protective breathing apparatus and a call was sent out for additional troops in protective suits with flame throwers. Since they didn't have any sort of protective gear for the cadaver dogs, they were sent back to the base camp as a precaution immediately after they alerted to the two small graves.

Juvenal and Jovian were hungry when they got back to Chanuck's cabin. They found the fixings for sandwiches in the kitchen. They prepared the meal in near silence; both were deep in thought of what had to be accomplished and what it would take for them to get it done. And, once they worked themselves into the state it would take to perform together what their cousin was metabolically able to do on his own, would they be able to return to themselves or be condemned to a life of seclusion as Chanuck was? Would they ever be able to live with their families again?

They started to hash out their plan and brought one of Chanuck's hunting dogs inside the cabin to try out their abilities to reenact his work. The dog was a gentle English Setter. Normally this was not the type of animal that needed Juvenal's calming talents, but today he was going to try to turn this wonderful pet into a raging beast whose pitch of rage would metamorphose Jovian's annoying dusty grey spores into lethal weapons.

The setter looked up at them, tail constantly wagging to match its toothy grin. Juvenal felt a pang of extreme guilt as he mentally sent messages of rage and hate to the animal the same way he had previously sent messages of calm and love to animals all his life. The dog began to look confused, its ears twitching back and down then up and inquiring, its tail had stopped wagging. Then a low and sinister sound began emanating from deep in its throat and its eyes began to narrow into slits. All of a sudden, Jovian was grateful that he had tethered the canine to the cast iron ring imbedded into the mortar of the fireplace.

"The poor thing seems ready for you, Jovian. I don't think it could be any angrier."

Jovian began to disrobe, grey dust starting to float in the air. Naked and looking as though he had just rolled in the remnants of a fire pit, he advanced toward the snarling dog. As he approached the setter, he slapped his hands together as if dusting them off in the animal's face. The dog's eyes flared open as if suddenly jarred by something and its ears went forward while it's brow furrowed deeply over the eyes. The eyes looked way into the distance just as they had seen Chanuck's eyes stare off. It had worked. The two man punch of the brothers had the apparent same effect as the single one man attack of their cousin. Obviously, the stories Popy told of his test runs of the capsules had been true and the fungi had metabolized in them in a lesser but useful way after all.

The only problem was of course that they couldn't turn off the effects on the dog and they couldn't get to the tether to release him outside. They would not chance another test inside the cabin and the dust was still floating in the air.

The brothers thought it might be wise to leave the cabin for some fresh air. When they went out on the porch a scent of burning brush mingled with the pine smell in the air. They could see smoke rising about four hundred yards away and could hear the muffled voices of many men and women seemingly yelling out orders and some words of panic.

The breathing masks were helping to deal with the smoke arising from the controlled burn of the dusty foliage along the way as well as the danger of the floating fungi. The air seemed to be getting thicker with it as they progressed and then they came to a startling sight. Before them, in an unnatural bowl in a large pine tree was what appeared to be a larger than life grey dusty "nest ball". It was definitely large enough to hold a very large animal or even a grown man.

The officers on point signaled a halt and regress of the troops in order to reconsider the situation. The scientists huddled near the edge of the clearing the old pine was in discussing the possibilities of what could be housed within the "nest ball". There were no known birds in their region or even in areas of the United States that would build such a structure and so close to the ground where it's young could be exposed to prey. It was, however, hard to imagine offspring requiring such a large habitat to be vulnerable to any known prey of that forest other than man himself. So still the question remained, "What could live in such a structure?"

All of a sudden, the "nest ball" began to sway with no wind in the trees and a crackling sound like dry hay being shredded could be heard. Then a hole started to form near the top and a human hand could be seen working its way through the latticed twigs.

It wasn't a woodland animal in the "nest ball", but a man with long muscular arms covered with the same grey spore dust.

The command was given to the Mounties and deputies to "stand ready and hold fire."

No one could immediately process what their eyes were seeing. After struggling through the entwined debris, before them eventually stood a well-muscled, seemingly healthy man of about thirty-five years old, apparently blinded by a grey film covering his eyes. His red hair was matted with dry leaves and spore dust and he bore his yellowed teeth seated in blackened gums. He let out hideous calls while staring ahead blindly into a place only his mind could see.

Everyone was in further awe because of the long moving hairs on certain parts of his body.

As they looked at him and he looked into his own netherworld, nerves became frayed and fingers began to twitch. No one wanted to kill an innocent man, but then again no one knew if they were facing a sane man and an insane one who could be dangerous.

"Sir, I am Dr. Ribeau, the vet from over near Cat Lake, and I'd like to help you if you'd let me. Can you see me, sir? I can come up to you alone and everyone else can wait here while I see what I can do for you, Sir." The man seemed to hear him, but only wagged his head from side to side like a blind man listening to music. "I've got a people doctor here too if you'd rather talk to her." No answer, just movement from one foot to the other. Then another of those wild crazy cries, worse than the sounds heard when he exited the "nest ball".

Everyone took a step back while the guns remained raised and ready.

Chanuck didn't answer or give any indication that he understood or even heard anything my dad had said to him.

My dad was good about giving me a full report of the events since it was my leads that eventually led to the take down. He figured that by twelve, I was old enough to handle the grisly details since I had already witnessed quite a lot with what had happened with Mother and Son and their victims. I took good notes of just how everything unfolded.

The flame thrower operators came up from behind with the muzzles of the weapons sparking and smoking. At this point, even the horses had been sent back up the trail for fear of a stampede to get away from the flames or even get infected by the fungi which were becoming more and more noticeable on the upper level florae.

A sample of the spores covering the outside of the nest ball had been delivered to the scientists at the back of the posse by a HazMat suited officer. While the tension grew among the officers surrounding the subject area, a report came forward that the sample analyzed was indeed identical to the spore matter involved in the crazed dogs and bobcats. It was also determined that a fungus from this sample was an older, more mature strain and most likely contained the parent spore.

Unintentionally self-infected with the spores his own body exuded, the carrier of the clan's hope for Canadian revenge suddenly displayed a look of extreme terror and made a beeline for the security of his nest.

The horde had come from nowhere. To Chanuck it seemed there were a hundred or more when actually there were less than fifty.

What were they...there were male and female? They had metal appendages attached to long limbs! Some had claws of fire! They walked upright to mimic him, to fool him - they were not like him. They were ... What? What was he?

They were so many! They could destroy his kind! What was his kind? He couldn't let his kind die out! He had to protect them from these wild invaders who were a danger to his own future and his clan's future. What were they?

He had to act. He had to get into his hiding place to think and decide how to protect everyone he knew.

The members of the troop had no idea whether this wild looking man in front of them had weapons he was reaching for in the "nest ball" or if he was only attempting to hide from them. The commander stepped forward again, "Sir, you are ordered to stop and stand fast." But the man thing only looked over his shoulder at him and snarled much like a cornered wild animal would. "Stop now sir or we will shoot!" However, this again was answered only by growls and unintelligible guttural language as he lept into his lofty domain.

Then there was rustling and snapping sounds as if something was breaking through the "nest ball" walls. The men could only imagine some weapon being thrust through the debris walls to fire at them.

The Mounties were rightfully on edge. They carried a heavy load on their training and abilities. There were a number of civilians in the posse who fell under their responsibility to protect as well as the entire province. From the information they had been given at the last briefing about this biological threat, they may well have been protecting the entire world. Tension among them was high and their weapons were held on the ready to respond to any sign of danger.

Chanuck had a walking stick of polished oak that he carried with him on hikes through his beloved woods during happier days. Today he used it to break through the mat walls of his protective nest to see the offending horde threatening his world.

Chanuck's walking stick broke through the matting.

The commander yelled, "Back field cover, front line fire!", as he leapt behind a boulder for cover, pulling my dad along with him. Unlike the colonial one shot then reload firing lines that ultimately defeated the British troops during the freedom fighting wars with the American Colonies, these troops were fully loaded, "full metal jacket" many times over. There was no need for them to drop and reload musket balls and use powder horns.

The "nest ball" began to literally disintegrate before their eyes.

"Gun! Gun!" was shouted out by one of the constables as the converted tree limb was mistaken for the barrel of a rifle.

My father himself was carrying his over-and-under, so he, along with everyone else who was armed, had begun to fire at the "nest ball", and fire and fire.

The shells and bullets bore into the "nest ball" and began to tear it apart, bit by bit with twigs and debris exploding into the air. Spore dust and cordite filled the air and the nostrils of everyone in the posse, in spite of the masks.

The disorientated man-animal inside of his nest became increasingly scared and confused, and then curled himself into a tight pre-natal type position. The next thing the pitiful, infected man-animal knew was intense pain and misery that the invading lead and buckshot inflicted on his body. Chanuck threw back his head and howled in pain and anger as his body was riddled. Blood poured from his wounds in a slow grayish red ooze like partially frozen tributaries merging into an equally slow river. The floor of the nest became gooey with his blood and the heavy layered spore dust.

The light went out in the eyes of the heir to the Canadian revenge plans for the wrongs done to the small village of Swovatni, Romania more than half a century ago as huge chunks of pine bark splintered into the mix.

The posse witnessed the utter disintegration of the "nest ball" and heard the last agonizing utterance of its inhabitant.

As the gun fire stopped and the remainder of the crazed man's habitat crumbled, the flame thrower troops were ordered to burn it all to ashes. As this was being done, a map of the forest was studied in order to locate the deceased offender's cabin. The land essayer's office had provided the exact coordinates filed on the land trust deed when Chanuck purchased the property. Their main concern was to destroy any possible fungi living in the home because of Chanuck residing there for many years.

Juvenal and Jovian were confused by the commotion that seemed to be rapidly approaching the cabin, but they felt nothing good could be involved with it. Again, they retreated into the house to figure things out. This was a trend that proved their undoing.

Inside the cabin, the previously gentle hound that the brothers had turned into a raging beast had been savagely straining at the leash that tethered it to the mortar which molded the river rocks into a fireplace wall. The metal ring that had been placed there over a century ago was slowly being wrenched loose.

The animal was filled with a rage that he couldn't even understand. All of his life he had been fed and treated really good by man. He had always loved man and man had loved him too. By all his senses he had known this, but now all he felt toward man was anger and hate, hate for the very human smell that permeated all of the air around him. He had always hunted with man, but now all he wanted to do was hunt man himself.

Not knowing how the animal's attitude had evolved inside the cabin, the brothers were overwhelmed by the frothy, grimacing canine that they faced as they slowly turned around from the wooden door at the horrifying sounds behind them. The dog was in front of them and the posse was getting closer outside behind them. Confusion was rampant.

The fear the brothers felt sent spores and psychic vibrations emanating from them into the air making the atmosphere in the cabin a lethal metabolic concoction that no post WWII amateur scientist could have ever imagined.

The insanity that this urged in the dumb beast gave it the final strength it needed to break the wrought iron tether ring free of the crumbling mortar. The animal charged, teeth bared, full speed head on, at Jovian, the larger of the two men. Its sharp canine fangs clenched firmly into the Mounty's neck and began to savagely wrench its own head from side to side as if it was trying to break the man's head clean off his body. Juvenal began screaming and fruitlessly trying to get his brother free from the beast's grip. Jovian could only gurgle and flail.

Outside the posse had reached the cabin yard and didn't know what to make of the voices and sounds escaping the house. The first thought in everyone's mind was that more dangerous men like the man in the "nest ball" were holed up inside. To them, everything they were hearing sounded just as inhuman as Chanuck had. The Commander ordered the flame-thrower armed officers to surround the structure and engulf it in flames. The fleet of firemen and tanker trucks that had been accompanying the posse in order to ward against an all-out forest fire came up behind them to control the intended burn.

The raging hound had been brought down by the large carving knife that Juvenal had found in the kitchen. With his excitement and efforts to save his brother's life, he had nearly severed the animal's head completely off. The whole incident had been long and hard fought, exhausting them both and Jovian was bleeding heavily as they dragged themselves toward the door.

Suddenly the brothers understood what they heard going on in the forest earlier but the awareness was far too late for it to do them any good. They realized now what the yells and screams and shouts had to have been. It was the demise of their cousin and with the roar of the flames surrounding the cabin, also the end of their efforts to fulfill the ancestors' wishes. They sat on the couch, held each other and cried, more out of disappointment in their failure than in fear of the fire.

The cabin walls were thick so accelerant was brought in to add to the mix and aid the flame throwers in bringing it all down to benign ashes. The growls and snarls had all ceased about ten minutes earlier, but with the roaring flames, only a six inch crawl space and no basement, it was certain that nothing and no one had escaped the building. The entire burn took more than two hours to complete and then the water tanks were brought up to wet it all down and alleviate any chance of the fire spreading.

A huge gravesite was dug by a piece of heavy equipment and the ashes from the "nest ball", the cabin, the unearthed dog corpses along with surrounding dirt, everything from the hunters' specimens, the scientists' samples (except for those archived by the CDC) and all evidence of what had transpired was buried six feet under in order to salvage the pristine recreational reputation that the province relied on so much.

Meanwhile, after exams of those posse members who had gone back to the base camp lab, the CDC scientists eased everyone's apprehensions by announcing that the excessive amount of cordite in the air had evidently negated the spores' ability to penetrate the nasal passages of those who inhaled them.

Everything was wrapped up and covered up. A press release was prepared with very careful and vague accounts of all that had transpired in the last twenty-four hours without making any connection to the campsite horror of the week prior or the contracting of the hunters.

The officials hoped that the accounting of the three cousins falling asleep in a beer stupor without replacing the fire screen in front of a roaring blaze they lit to keep warm would hold up with the gypsy family who had lost part of their clan's future. The families were presented with beautiful urns, sealed and said to be filled with their loved one's ashes.

The scorched woods were kept closed by the Provincial Forestry Department in order to restore its natural beauty as soon as possible.

The press was expected to accept these printed, hurriedly handed out statements, but someone was not content with them. Other more suspicious statements about the happenings in the Manateau Province were leaked out to certain sympathizers by someone who worked for a certain local official. Members from F.A.M.S., For All Mammals to be Safe, and N.F.P., Natural Forests Preserved, were asking for explanations of e-mails and pictures they received anonymously.

Suspicions were being raised everywhere and connections were being made between the American and Canadian instances coming so close, nearly overlapping each other. The genie was getting harder to keep in the bottle. No one noticed the tall reporter with the long curly red hair and the video recorder he had secreted under his vest.

DESERTION INTO TERROR

The soldiers were everywhere in town, but could they have still been considered soldiers after they had deserted their posts? In the middle of the night, the village was awakened by rapid firing of M1 Garand's. People sleepily left their homes in robes and coats hastily thrown over nightshirts. Children cried and huddled behind adults looking for protection and reassurance.

Fourteen American and Canadian soldiers herded everyone into the town square at gun point. One of the village aldermen raised his objections and was shot down immediately without warning or remorse. Women screamed, men swore, more children cried and barking dogs were also shot without care.

The deserters declared the town sequestered and warned that more of their comrades would be arriving and that the citizens were to show them the same respect and obedience that they were now being taught. The two cells of the constable's small building only held eight persons each and that is where they held the men that were used to bring in crops and slaughter hogs and chickens for food. The rest of the men were restrained by chains padlocked around forest trees until they were needed. The able bodied women and most children were housed in the inn rooms above the tavern.

Little attention was paid to the older women who fled into the caves outside of town. Little did the villainous soldiers know, but those were the townsfolk they should have guarded the most. They were the medicine women and alchemists of the tribe and highly respected by everyone. In the frightened hearts of the then imprisoned village, they knew those women would be their best hope.

They took with them three very special young children that they would have given their lives to protect. They were the identical "triplets" that the village considered its good luck charms. No crops had failed or been too small in the ten years since they were born. Every calf had come in alive and healthy and all of the chickens laid lots of big eggs. The town had grown since the year the boys had been born. They were pre-teens when the deserters brought the Second Great War to this small Romanian township and they were young men when the people sent them out to seek revenge.

As word got out about this cowards' hide out, more and more unsavory characters began showing up at the town limits. The free world was in the fight of its life so no one took notice of the pain and suffering happening in this small corner of the European countryside. Men who refused to buckle down under the illegal regime or who tried to protect their women and even children from the sexual and mental abuse the criminals inflicted, were mercilessly shot as examples of the consequences of disobedience. The people began to feel that even God had abandoned them.

It was this sense of hopelessness that drove them deep into alternative methods that put most of their souls at the devil's doorstep.

The crime leveled on the small tribe went on for years and recovery took its village generations to regain its population. The means to seek revenge on the nations that allowed such beasts to wreak that devastation took years to develop. But the very patience that allowed the townsfolk to quietly wait for the medicine women and alchemists to complete their research would also give them the ultimate generational satisfaction they craved.

They would release upon those nations the worse and most lethal DNA the world could ever imagine.

LINEAL DILUTION

Rowaena Seldowsky lived in the Mid South Region of the Eastern United States. Her ancestor had migrated to the States sometime after WWII.

It had taken him and everyone else who survived the pillaging by the deserters who ruined their village quite a few years to recover from the harsh life they had to scrounge up after the cowards were brought down. Officials never blamed the elders for the potions they created that were slowly worked into the marauders' food to eventually bring them to their just rewards. And no one asked for a final body count or survivor tally of the horrible men who had done so many horrid acts.

The town women were able to keep most of the children alive through the ordeal, but afterward had to work in severe housing conditions to raise them to a point where they had developed enough to fend for themselves. And fortunate for them all, the "triplets" were among the survivors. While the younger women worked the fields and rebuilt the cottages with the few surviving men, the older women toiled with their potions and herbs and chemicals to formulate the means by which they would seek the tribe's pay back.

It had taken 8 years of research, countless sacrificed animals and grueling experiments on the handful of murdering deserters that weren't killed outright by the survivors, yet who no one looked for after the carnage, but were kept deep down in the caves north of the village. The deadly means by which the gypsies would make sure America and Canada paid for the cruelties inflicted on them for years was finally ready.

When the women first began seeking justice for the suffering of their families and loved ones deep in the belly of the great cave warren, their first thoughts were of undetectable poisons that could be secreted into the villains' food and drinks. However, as more and more of the clan was decimated and the very existence of the people's bloodline became threatened, the quest began to reach out to destroy the future of the motherlands responsible for such vile men.

The village's golden children, the red headed "triplets" had shown signs of being special from the moments of their births. They were all born on the same night, in the same village, three streets apart to three separate unrelated teen mothers. None of the girls were really old enough to take on the role of motherhood and they admitted to being impregnated by one donor but would not confess as to who the father was. However, as the boys grew their identical paternal blood line was obvious in the fact that they exhibited strikingly identical facial features and hair color. The tribe dubbed the boys "the triplets"

The young mothers all died during the night of a full moon three months apart before the "triplets" reached the age of two. At a communal meeting, it was agreed that the three should be put under the care and development of the shaman women. "These boys are suspicious by their births", said the clan leader, "It is not wise to adopt them out to average families and we don't want to lose them to the authorities." A vote was cast and the women took on the responsibility of their young charges.

And it came to be that the village alchemists and medicine women felt that the revenge sought by their people would best be carried out through the hands and descendants of the phenomenal three.

While tending to the boys who remained hidden in one of the many chambers of the great cave, one of the younger apprentices noticed something odd among the debris and guano littering the deeper cave floors - bat caucuses and bones. The remains didn't seem to have resulted from natural causes of death because the carcasses were rended and crushed. What had done so much damage to the bats was worrisome and from the amount of debris, the killers were many.

In the caves, bats didn't have natural enemies and the women and boys were certainly nothing the flying mammals had to worry about. As far as anyone knew, there were no other creatures at this subterranean level. The apprentice ran to call an elder because she sensed something was very wrong and nothing could be allowed to be wrong near "the three".

The apprentice found the head shaman and reported her discovery, "Mam, there is something frightening at the back of the cave.", and she told her the reason for her concern. Bats were important, they controlled the insect population and living in a wilderness environment like the cave, insect control was an important item that warranted attention. If something was needlessly killing an unnecessary number of bats, the women might have needed to take some sort of action.

The elder snatched up another lantern and the two headed deeper into the abyss with only cooking knives for defense. There was one other thing that was seriously quizzical - the lack of footprints or tracks in the debris. Then they considered that the problem could be rabid bats, which could be dangerous for everyone, so they moved on slowly, careful not to startle the overhead cloud of bats.

Movement near the cave ceiling got their attention as something that appeared to be white ruffled what seemed like it's wings. The women slowly raised their lanterns for a better inspection.

While other brown fuzzy bodies huddled in large masses, a handful of grayish white animals angrily crawled over them rending their hides and pulling apart and chewing off wings, legs and heads of the defenseless creatures. It was nearly as horrendous a sight as they had witnessed on the bloody streets down in the village. The terrorizing animals were larger than the regular bats, yet seemed bat-like and they were covered with some sort of grey fuzz.

The women backed out of the chamber and went to discuss everything they had witnessed with the others. The look, size, and behavior of these new specimens were extremely alarming and interesting at the same time.

It was decided that they would capture and study some of the unusual animals. Since they moved so slowly and were so intent on attacking the defenseless bat colony, it was easy to knock them down by simply throwing large stones at them.

The semi conscious animals were then tied down on makeshift examining boards. After close study, the grey coating on the large powerful bodies proved to be a sort of mold with very dense spores. Despite being covered by the fungi, the wicked little creatures appeared to be in otherwise good health. The only thing out of the ordinary about these bats in relation to the regular ones was their seemingly insane killing mental attitude.

Since the animals weren't sick, the first two women handled the grey bats with bare hands. However, soon they found their hands covered with pulsating blisters that erupted into oozing blisters inching up their forearms. The pain and conditions rendered their hands useless so they were drenched with alcohol and bandaged to the elbows to try and stop the spreading infection.

One of the sister alchemists was in the finishing stages of her medical studies in Berlin when the war broke out. Aneya chose to return home two years later to be available to give any aid her people might need. Little did anyone know how bad the village would need her capabilities.

The grey bats were kept in isolation cages and only fed or handled with work gloved hands and long sleeves. The affected women's health got increasingly worse. The flesh under the bandages was being eaten away and the stench given off nauseated even them. They ran a fever so high that it was blamed for bringing them to the brink of madness. Later it was found that the fever was only partially the reason for their decline in sanity.

One of the spore covered flying mammals was female and gave birth soon after being captured but the viciousness of the pups as they were being whelped was frightening. As they were emerging from the birth canal, they began ravenously biting and tearing at the mother's legs and at each other. They were covered with the spores when they emerged, so it seemed they were born with the fungi as a natural coating. None of the new born animals exhibited the sores that were festering on the humans that had come in contact with the mold. Neither did they have the extreme rise in body temperature or emanating odor as the women.

Aneya noted that though the spore covered bats crawled over the normal bats as they rended them, they did not transfer the coating to them. It was obvious to her that this condition in the bats was genetic not infectious within the species, but obviously infectious to other species of life as she watched the infected women's deterioration into death.

The researchers started to look more closely into the spores to determine if there was any generational change in the coatings on the pups and the adult grey bats. An experiment was conducted where two small rodents were exposed one each to an adult and one to a pup. The exposed animals both showed signs of infection, however the rodent exposed to the adult showed signs the next day while the one exposed to the pup was blistering within ten hours. This awakened questions in Aneya and the group saw this as a road to investigate and also to document.

Eric, another college graduate who was a journalist with a large newspaper in Berlin, returned to support his clan. He got out his typewriter and began Volume One, he would be the Swovatni people's official scribe.

The trial and error research went on for the next seven and one half years. With help from the few remaining village men, all of the grey bats were trapped and caged. Some of the brown bats were also caught to use as lab subjects along with rabbits, squirrels, a few dogs and the seven captured and imprisoned deserters. Those women and their lab work were well in advance of most research of their time. They purposely reproduced more of the grey bats and discovered varying evolution of the fungus. They were able to manipulate the intensity and variation of the spores and their affect on other living organisms.

Eric began typing on Volume Two. The first book detailed the questions that arose from intense observation and the second book would lay out the results of years of trial and error work.

The time passed, the work continued and the drive stayed alive. The entire tribe was of one mind, the retaliation on the sons and daughters and grandchildren of the men who had so savagely tried to annihilate the clan's future heirs. Some of the women and young girls raped and abused by the evil cowards would never be able to bear the children needed in order to restore the village's population. This resulted in the dilution and hybridization of the tribe's bloodlines. It was necessary to offer gifts and livestock to other villages in order for the Swovatni tribe's surviving teen boys and young men to court and marry their unbetrothed females of child bearing age.

It was decided that the research would not stop until the product sent out into the world to exact payback from their enemies would reach into the future of these countries and attack them when they least expected. In this manner, no one would be able to imagine where the attack was launched from and their tribe would be the only ones to secretly relish the victory. This entire plan was envisioned by Aneya as she quietly took on the role of second shaman in command. She privately regretted not being able to return to Berlin to pursue her medical career and, though she arrived after the carnage, harbored as much hate, if not more, than anyone else in the small township.

The origin of the lethal spores on the grey bats was never determined, but it didn't matter because the fungus that finally evolved through the patience, genius, engineering and diligent work of the best minds of Swovatni, Romania was far better and programmable then the original genus discovery.

The fungus would attack the creators of evil in three ways and each design would be carried out of the country by "the triplets" whom they all loved.

One strain was infective from man to animal - mammal to mammal; the second was infective from man to animal - mammal to avian; and the third would be the most directly infective from spore to man - infection by touch.

The lab subjects had been injected and rejected and infected until the desired means of spreading and manipulating the most manic mentality resulted in both mankind and animal species through contact with these fungi was finally accomplished.

The first spore exuded from the pores of a healthy male pumped full of excitement and hate would drift into the inquisitive nostrils of the very animals that rich American and Canadian households considered "family members" and that were even allowed to sleep in their beds. This meant their beloved pets could even devour them in the night. The fools also slept and camped out in the wilderness where those beasts' wild cousins roamed and where the grey dust would spread in their systems as animal after animal greeted and sniffed each other.

The next spore passed on by human perspiration that would dry to reveal the grey dust on clothing and bedding. It was engineered to adhere to bird feathers, then fall off while the fowl was in flight and attach to any mammal's hairs at which time the spore dust would start a chemical reaction akin to acid erosion that would eat down into the skin of the mammal's body. This would inflict excruciating pain and confusion. The most important thing about those spores was that they did not wash off with anything; they just constantly ate into the body causing and increasing madness. However, neither of these genetically engineered spores could pass on through females metabolisms, but were unmistakably inherited by males.

The third genus of spore was indeed the most exciting for Aneya and her lab mates. These stayed on human skin and transferred by touch more like the original grey bat fungi to infect human beings directly. However, these spores incorporated a number of symptoms that were never inflicted by the initial grey bat carriers. Besides the open pustules and foul odor, they also produced wild hair growth, guttural speech, ravenous appetite, thirst for blood, unstable gait, extreme anger and irrational insanity. A simple touch, scratch, or bite would spread this physical disaster from person to person in remarkable time. And the best way to transfer those spores was human skin to human skin.

Eric had nearly finished typing Volume Three which had the written generational instructions for bestowing the tribe's revenge on those who left his people in so much pain.

It was time for the books to be bound, so the alchemists made the glue and one of the tribal taxidermists tanned the hide of one of the deserters after his lab use was ended and the leather covers were designed and lettered in gold leaf.

The "MAN TO ANIMAL" spores produced were packaged in capsule form for the purpose of being ingested by the youngest son of the second or third generation males of the middle and oldest of "the three", just before entering puberty. It had to be timed before the year 2000 in order for the spores to be metabolized into the young boys and be fully effective by the time the boys became young men during the first thirteen years of the next millennium. All of the infections were to be initiated in 2013- seventy years after the start of the Swovani invasion. It was intended that the number thirteen would be very unlucky for America and Canada.

With gloved hands, a section of human hide was rolled over and over again in the "MAN TO MAN" spore then along with the third set of volumes was placed in a glass box with brass frames and a small brass lock. The box was then covered in paraffin and instructions were taped to the box with a severe warning, "DO NOT OPEN THIS BOX UNTIL 2002, ALL VOLUMES HAVE BEEN READ, THE VOLUME THREE INSTRUCTIONS ARE TO BE FOLLOWED EXACTLY ELEVEN YEARS LATER." The vengeance of the glass box was to be bestowed upon the nations by the youngest male descendant of the youngest member of "the three" in the generation of the new millennium. It was generally thought that if all others failed, the youngest of the youngest would surely survive to complete the mission.

It took three more months for Eric to type two more original sets of the volumes. There was just enough human leather for them all to be bound. The deserter who's hide had been used had been an extremely tall man with an exceptionally large girth. Each of "the three" was given a set of the three volumes. "From our males because of your males on all of your kin.", was the last statement scribed in Volume Three of each set.

Eric was proud of his part in the cause and signed off with a flurry in beautiful penmanship at the end of each volume, "Eric the Writer."

The townsfolk sold what they cold to finance the long journeys ahead for the young men. The elders chose locations in which as many heavily populated zones as possible could be affected and where many people were thought to travel in and out of frequently.

The oldest carrier of revenge was sent to establish his family on the east coast of the United States; the middle carrier was sent to set up life in Canada near Toronto; and the youngest was told to begin his future in the western area of the U.S. The time after WWII was still an era when people homesteaded a territory and remained there for generations. However, times changed and people became more mobile and lives were driven by job availability and suburban growth.

So, though "the three" married and set the plan into motion where it was thought to have the most powerful effect, their children and grandchildren moved about and started their own lives in various locations. But, like sleeper cells planted by political enemies of those nations, the clan's sacrificing, plans, and thirst for revenge were kept alive in the hearts of the descendants of "the three". By the time the youngest male grandchild of each man who was sent forth reached high school graduation the engineered metabolic change was under way and the three sets of the volumes were in the right hands to set off the pay back for the Swovatni Tribe's lineal dilution.

But the once proud tribe and devastated village was never able to fully regain its territorial footing. Generational changes, familial integration and urban sprawl had swallowed the once proud township into becoming a mixed income subdivision of Berlin style townhouses and two story apartment complexes. The caves and laboratories had long since been dismantled and closed by a man-made avalanche and the remaining fungi had long ago been destroyed by fire to prevent local contamination.

The revenge that was put into play over half a century ago was in the hands of the few 21st Century descendants that lived in another hemisphere far, far away.

Rowaena was one of these grand-descendants and knew well what was expected of her and her siblings. Though it was her little brother's responsibility to carry out the legacy of revenge, it was his siblings' duty to see he made it to the fulfillment of his commitment. She wasn't so sure that she believed in the tribe's revenge as much as her two sisters and her baby brother did. He had been all pumped up about how important he was to the family ever since his eleventh birthday when Dad had made such a big thing about him and their Canadian cousin swallowing those capsules. But so much time had passed since that horrible time, Roweana wondered if anyone was still alive who could actually reap the reward of the payback. In America pure blood lines weren't that important anymore and no one she knew had ever spoken to anyone who lived through that time of suffering, anyway.

Ivan hadn't exactly lived the life of someone carrying an entire tribe's legacy. He didn't turn out to be one of the princes the tribe dreamed the grandsons of "the three" would be. It was time for him to carry out his mission, but instead of being at home in Tennessee preparing himself, he was in a jail in Georgia for the next three years for passing bad checks. This was something the clan could never have fathomed in the early fifties when hardly anyone in Swovatni even had checking accounts.

If anything good could be found in Ivan's situation it was that he was in prison for a nonviolent offense and was a model prisoner, so in turn he was allowed a few liberties, one of which was smoking on the roof deck and having a roof top garden. His revenge mission was to infect the avian population in order for them to spread the villainous spores from the air. Ivan had a solid plan to get it done.

While tending his plants on the roof deck, he noticed the large number of hawks hunting in the surrounding woods and that the small raptors' favorite meal was rodents. Fortunately for Ivan, the prison was full of mice and rats. He presented a plan to the warden to rid the place of the vermin and was given privileges in the prison workshop to build the traps he outlined in his plan. What Ivan lacked in lawful behavior, he was rich of in devious endeavors. Soon he had a steady job of rodent control for the lockup.

No one knew what he did with the mice and since he didn't work in the galley, no one cared. Most of the screws teased him about using them for fertilizer. However, in essence, Ivan was building a better trap with the mice than he had designed for the mice. If he couldn't get out to the birds he would bring the birds to him. No one was ever interested in what he was doing on the roof since it topped a seven story building with twelve foot ceilings and straight outer walls, no windows, and had no fire stairs so it offered Ivan no means of escape. But he wasn't concerned with escaping, he was however obsessed with fulfilling his birthright mission.

Using the plump mice as irresistible tasty bait, the hawks were enticed into one way traps themselves. After a few good treats, he released them. Soon the birds lose their fear of him and the cages and were literally racing each other to enter the traps knowing they would be fed. His plan was to gain the confidence of the fowl, then infect them with the spores he was collecting from his own body in his cell. He was working on attracting as many birds as he felt would be necessary to inflict panic and suffering all at once over a large area without warning before the authorities could figure out how the disease was spreading. Genetic manipulation had rendered his kinfolk immune to the spores so his plan to use large powerful birds that flew over heavily populated cities as well as far ranging farmland and forest areas seemed unstoppable.

His sister had told him about the failed attempts of their cousins to catch the powerful countries off guard. It didn't matter how the media attempted to camouflage the events, it was the timing and the areas and the numbers affected that lead them to speculate on exactly what had really happened. And they had been in touch with some of their Canadian cousins. They had grown apart from the mid-western clan relatives and obviously that family branch had lost track of the initial plan. If they hadn't, the bookstore would never have become so evident a threat. Ivan had no intention of allowing his attack to fail and he felt he had covered all of his bases. He had covered all of his scenarios from all angles except one he never saw coming.

Roweana loved her life in America and had been fortunate enough to have visited Romania in 1994 during a college trip through Europe. She saw the people and the land of her grandfather's family though she wasn't able to locate any living relatives. Maybe if she had met someone who could have awakened the spirit of revenge in her or if there had even been some sort of plaque commemorating the survival or sorrowing the great loss of the village but she had only the hatred and words of her very old great grandfather who claimed to have been one of the beloved "triplets". And even that story of him being one of the "mysterious babies" fell short in her opinion.

So the more Rowaena thought of her brother's plans to wreak devastation on innocent American lives, the more she felt obligated to put an end to generationally planned evil. Since the cousins had been stopped, her brother was the last and only male of her branch of the Swovatni tribe to reach puberty before the 21st century and since he had not bothered to stop his swindling life long enough to marry and bear a son of his own, Ivan was the last threat to what she loved.

Rowaena went to visit her brother at the prison. The visitation policies were liberal. Friday evenings and all day Saturdays and Sundays anyone could ask for an appointment to visit a loved one.

She did love her brother and she knew a lot of pressure had been brought upon him to fulfill the tribe's plot for revenge, but he didn't know that he was striving to complete a mission that had little meaning any more. She figured that if she spoke with Ivan about the changes back in Europe and how only a small bronze plaque remained dedicating the new subdivision to the old village that deteriorated there twenty-five years ago, she might be able to change his mind about the senseless mission of people long gone.

However, when her brother entered the visitation lounge and she looked into his face, she knew she had made the trip in vain. As he sat down across from her, she could see he was bursting with excitement and seemed to have a lot he wanted to say. "It's almost time you know. I've got it all figured out and I should have it all ready real soon. I've got the hawks as tame as hand-raised parakeets and they flock to the roof every evening just at dusk. I've even gotten the first ones to bring others. There are more than forty of them now and you can tell most have traveled from far away, but I feed them well when they come. This old pen has the fattest mice and rats I've ever seen. Those birds almost seem to love me, not one of them fly's away when I go out up there. "My calming telepathy is working on them even better than it worked on the screws.", he blurted out in a harsh whisper.

That was when Rowaena Seldowsky knew saving her precious life in America was going to mean betraying the brother she also loved. She had to weigh whether she could live with that, giving up one life to save, she couldn't even guess, how many more.

Then Ivan said, " I been saving up the dust in my blanket under my bunk. I need to save some more then all I got to do is go up in the middle of that roof and give it a good shake, then tell my birds to fly home. They'll drop and spread my wild spores all over the good south and pay them back for all they did to our people. When my fungi start eating into the flesh of every animal they touch, the madness will never end."
The look in his eyes was more frightening then any fear she had ever felt before.

She finished her visit with her brother and knew she had to do something. She hadn't been able to get in a word with him going on and on about the hawks and his power over them. He talked about how exciting it was to hand feed a live mouse to a wild predator. She grew sick of his sinister enjoyment in the cruelty of it all.

She asked to talk to the warden.

She was told that without an appointment, it would be at least an hour before the warden could see her and that he could give her only a few minutes of his busy schedule. Speaking to him was important so she told the receptionist she would definitely wait.

As she sat on the hard wooden bench in the hallway outside the warden's office, she tried to put together the words she needed to explain this seventy year plan of mayhem and murder. She had been raised with this tale of revenge and punishment being retold over and over again in order to be instilled in each generation. Now Rowaena had to find the right words to make it all believable to a stranger in one short meeting.

She could tell by the look in Warden Hollis' eyes that her story was falling on unbelieving ears. "Ms. Seldowsky, I know you have concerns about your brother's welfare, but believe me it is too late in the game to try for a plea of insanity. There's nothing wrong with Ivan and he serves a great purpose here as our exterminator. He's doing a good job and will leave here with a glowing reference when he is released."

She'd tried to alert him of the danger her brother presented without actually telling him the whole story of her family's wicked plans to make America and Canada pay for evil deeds done over seventy years ago. The general public didn't have good opinions about Gypsies as it was and she didn't want to fuel those feelings.

Rowaena realized that preventing her brother from destroying the country she loved was going to be totally up to her. She wasn't sure how she would get it done, but she knew she had to do it.

Ivan was almost ready to put his plan in action. He had built up so much spore dust in his blanket that it was heavy with them and he realized it was going to be rather difficult to manage. There was no way he could have folded it into a easily carried form and get it from his cell on level three to the roof of the seven story complex. He had to delve deeper into his devious self to come up with a solution.

He needed an excuse to use one of the large utility carts that the kitchen crew used to bring in goods from the grocery and supply delivery trucks. So, he started to hatch a plan.

The maintenance on the building was generally good and Ivan had to hatch a believable problem that he would be more than happy to take care of. So he decided to rely on his history of hopping from one job to another to help him do just that. About seven years ago he had worked as a laborer for a local roofing company until he got caught stealing shingles after hurricane winds had created a lot of roof work. He had peaked at his file when his good prisoner reputation gained him his first trustee job cleaning offices. Under job experience it only referred to his time with that company as "roofing work", not simply "laborer" which was actually all that he did while he worked there other than steal.

Ivan pried up a few shingles over the seventh floor storeroom and poured just enough water from a plastic jug he sneaked out of the kitchen to stain the ceiling. Then he poured a small puddle on the floor. It was in that storeroom that he kept his rat traps for that floor. Of course he was the one to discover the leak and offered to fix it in the interest of saving the Warden's funding more strain. And of course he would need to borrow a cart to carry all the tools he needed up to the roof. This also gave him a reason to get permission to use the service elevator. His cell wasn't far from it and he could manage to get his blanket that far. Once it was on the roof, it was his plan to tie it down tight enough to spring the spores into the air and onto the birds as he went about his regular routine of feeding them. He had a good supply of rodents cached away and was ready to put the final phase of his plan in motion.

Soon the predestined revenge of his ancestors would be fulfilled and he would have lived up to his mission in life. Rowaena had given him a disposable cell phone which he kept hidden away on the roof. He was ecstatic when he called her to say he was about to succeed in his tribe's plan.

She tried to play it casually and told him she was proud of his commitment to his lineage, which was a true statement since Ivan had never committed himself to anything but himself in his life. Never a job, never a sweetheart, never a friend, never an immediate family member, not even her, came before Ivan and himself. So it was no surprise to her that he had no allegiance to a country that gave his modern day family so much to live by and to live for. There was no more question in her mind or in her heart as to what had to be done and it was also evident that no amount of talking was going to change Ivan's mind or his planned actions.

She had only herself to depend on and she had to act and act fast. So, as she headed back to the prison, she dialed the penitentiary's visitor phone line to put in a request to see her brother. When she arrived, she was admitted without any hesitation because she was well known from her frequent visits to see her brother. She took the stairs straight up to the roof. She had just called him and found out he was up there coaxing the hawks right now. His plan to get his spore covered blanket onto the roof had succeeded and he was thrilled that she would be there to witness the culmination of his mission.

She knew it had to be the end of more than this mission. Ivan would never be deterred from doing what he had been told all his life was his and his alone to do. Roweana often thought about the course of her brother's life and wondered if maybe his family invoiced destiny was what had kept him from starting a family. She thought his fear of losing such a prominent tribal position to a younger heir of his own led to his solitary lifestyle and that lonely life ultimately led him to illegal mischief.

No one ever knew what personalities might develop in future generations. Ivan's personally had turned out to be an extremely self-centered one, yet was seriously lacking in self-confidence. Unfortunately he felt the mission to reek revenge on America was the sole purpose he had in life and despite his knack for resolving any obstacles to that end, he hadn't accomplished any other useful goal in his lifetime.

Roweana loved her job in the library of the Jones County Community College, loved her townhouse in old town, thought she might have a future with Terrance who she'd been dating for the last six months and whose hair was almost as red as hers, but loved her country more than anything else. She knew that America had been good to her family in spite of the tribe's old world small minded attitude and that they hadn't received as much of the mean bias that gypsies experienced in some other countries, all things considered. She would do what she felt she had to do to save the people of this country even if no one ever knew the sacrifice she was about to make.

In spite of it all, she loved her brother dearly and since her mother lost her bout with cancer and her father couldn't live without her, she and Ivan were all that was left of her great grandfather's son's descendants. His daughter's descendants were many, but being a female, she passed on to them the immunity to the spore effects only, not the lineal dilution to launch the revenge. Roweana could not produce spores and would see to it that those Ivan had produced would be destroyed.

Even though the warden did not believe the ancestral story she'd related to him, she wrote it all down and made explicit references to the suspicious happenings in the Mid-West and Canada and included references to the internet articles and emails that were leaked out. She also included instructions for and the importance of destroying all of the spores and sterilizing Ivan's cell and the entire rooftop and access points. She included a note that the influence on the birds under her brother's mental control would be neutralized once Ivan's thoughts were silent.

She realized that her last statement made her intentions seem premeditated, but she was sure her brother would not give up his mission easily and she was just as determined to stop his mission. She made sure that Warden Hollis would not see the folder with this information until nothing could be done to stop her from stopping Ivan.

Ivan had made his way to the roof with the utility cart containing his heavily spore laden blanket. As usual, no one paid any attention to what he was doing and just trusted that he could be relied on to actually be mending the leak on the roof, never guessing that Ivan had created the leak to camouflage his real intentions.

He had the blanket laid out in the center of the roof, suspended tightly between eight pegs hammered into five gallon cans of vegetables. The cans were stuck to the roof with the epoxy that was supposed to be used to repair the roof. He was going to use the tension in the blanket to propel the spores into the air as the hawks and eagles came to feed, and he had two cages packed with squirming food.

Roweana stepped out of the stairwell door and felt pangs of fear and panic. She had thought that she would have more time. Her brother was poised on the ledge of the roof with two fat wiggling mice in each hand by the tails. He was already calling the birds and his means of contamination was set up and ready to infect. If just the first four predators got dusted with the lethal fungi, an unimaginable amount of innocent people would get harmed. She heard the squawk of the incoming birds. There was no time to think, she had to react immediately to save her beloved country.

"God forgive me and give me strength," was all Ivan heard cried out before he felt a jolt and arms clasping around him as he and someone else were propelled forcibly over the edge of the seven story roof. The flailing rodents flipped helplessly through the air as Ivan flung them loose and unsuccessfully attempted to loosen the arms squeezing the life from him.

However, in less than ten seconds both Ivan and his attacker fatally plunged into the pavement.

The perimeter guard's canine partner began excitedly barking as they rounded the corner to the north quadrant. It took the guard a moment to realize what they had come upon. When he did, he immediately sounded an alert.

Since the prison had no windows, the logical source of the carnage on the ground outside the prison walls was the roof. Having been informed of the bloody horror, the Warden instantly thought of Ivan, his best prisoner, so he accompanied the guards to where everyone new had to be the origin of the event.

The stairwell door was always unlocked since an attempted escape by Ivan was never a concern and no one ever wanted to really know exactly what he was doing with the vermin he ridded the jail of. Today, however, the door was blocked by something heavy.

When Roweana had walked out onto the roof, Ivan was so preoccupied with calling the birds that he didn't realize he was no longer alone. She took advantage of the time to move some of the heavy bags of soil for his roof top garden in front of the large door. She hadn't meant to prevent entry to the roof, but only to effectively slow down anyone who would prevent her from doing what had to be done. Ivan had to be stopped.

With a few stiff armed efforts, the guards pushed open the stairwell door to the roof and, with Warden Hollis in the lead, walked out into the open. The first thing they noticed was the briefcase of files Roweana had compiled for them to realize the reasoning behind her actions and for the authorities to connect the dots in order to prevent the fruitless mission from being fulfilled.

The warden and the guards took in the scene on the roof, the cages of rodents, the outstretched dusty looking blanket, and so many large hawks and eagles in all of the surrounding trees. He walked to the north edge of the roof and looked down at the joined bodies nearly one hundred feet below.

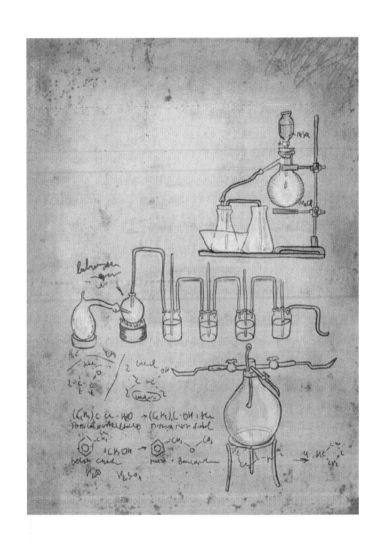

106

REVENGE & PERSEVERANCE

Only the spores would be effective as a weapon. Only the descendants of "the three" could weaponize the fungi other than the touch spores which were weapons from the start. Only the youngest males of the new millennium were effective in doing that.

All of the effective male lineage in the Western Hemisphere was dead. All of the hope for revenge on America and Canada was gone.

Aneya and the shaman women had worked so hard. They never wanted their work to be in vain. Aneya had secret plans of her own.

She had sons, also, and all of them had their father's red curly hair. A gene that was strong throughout all of his descendants. Years of laboring in a damp moldy research lab set up in an ancient cave took a toll on her health. Aneya never lived to see her grandchildren, but she would have known them in a crowd.

Aneya had sent her four youngest males of the seven children that she had given life to live with relatives of their father in the West. Two of the boys were identical twins who favored her except for the red locks and two strongly favored their father and the original "triplets". They were given instructions to be handed down through her descendants. She was always one to believe in a back-up plan. If the tribe's plan failed, her children would see that her desire for justified revenge would be put into play.

The doctor/scientist would be proud to know that her red-headed clan was all in place in the new millennium.

LINEAL STRENGTH

The call came at 5:15pm on the land line phone. Everyone carried cell phones but only family members knew the number on this line. With the crazy weather that seemed so hard to predict this millennium, no one could tell when the power might fail and only land lines worked without electricity.

All that was said was, "You're on". The same call was made at 5:20pm and then again five minutes later, and five minutes after that, on three other hard wired phones in three separate locations across the Western Hemisphere. The Elder of the American clan knew what must be done next.

Each of the redheaded middle aged men immediately went to his hiding place to retrieve the family heirloom that had been entrusted to his care. One went to the attic, one to the basement, the third to the garage, and fourth to his workshop. The four cases they lovingly cared for were over fifty years old and seemed light for their size. They were identical and each was actually a box, in a box, in a box with the inner most box wrapped in what was the most secure plastic wrap for that time.

As the men had been instructed from the first year they began to enter puberty, the cases had been protected but never opened. It had also been stressed how important these boxes were to realizing the vengeance that must be sought for the wrong that was done to their very wonderful grandmother who sacrificed so much for their clan.

They never got to know her in the flesh because she never left Swovatni, Romania but they knew her through pictures their fathers so lovingly displayed on family room walls wherever they lived.

Their fathers had related the story many, many times because they were never to forget what was done to their people's village so horrendously over half a century ago. Restitution had to be made and the collection plates were in their hands. Obviously, by the calls, their American and Canadian cousins had all failed and the responsibility for the Gypsy tribe's revenge rested on their heads.

The four red headed middle aged men did not all live in the same city, state, or country. As their fathers and the "triplets" before them, they were spread out to inflict the most damage possible to the descendants of the men who attempted to wipe out their ancestors and make their own existence impossible.

Being the exceptional scientist their grandmother had been, she had prepared her own sons to carry out the punishment that had to be dealt on America and Canada. These were the very countries that had bred the evil cowards who had tried to destroy their clan's future and caused the need for this lineage of perseverance and revenge.

Aneya had been a brilliant medical student and had been accepted as a researcher in a fine hospital in Berlin when these horrific acts were carried out. When she secretly returned home to help her people free themselves of the invaders, Aneya thought she would return to Berlin and take up the life that had been laid out for her. But the evil men did not leave the captured village at the end of World War II. Since they had deserted their Commands, they could not return to the very countries that had spawned them without incurring prosecution.

However, no one came to punish them for what they did in Swovatni. No one came to free the tribe. No one took notice, no one cared. So the villagers who survived the marauders took it upon themselves to destroy them and regain their freedom.

They vowed to seek revenge on the lands that had birthed them. Aneya and her shaman sisters set out to find a way to make them pay. Though the original weaponized spores had been put into play to effect warm blooded living humans and animals that would wreak havoc, work continued on the spore genes to use them even more extensively and stealthily.

The redheaded man with the fuzzy red beard had come into the village on the back of an Arabian stallion. It was obvious that he would draw a lot of attention in a small settlement of olive complected gypsies and the horse added to his mystery. He was about six feet tall and built like a well-muscled man that worked hard for his living, with perfect white teeth.

He went straight to the constable's cabin and knocked before walking in. He spoke with a European ascent which was hard to tie to a particular border. There was a deserted court house building at the opposite end of the village's main inroad and the stranger was interested in acquiring it.

The bearded stranger said he was a bookkeeper, which belied what his physique suggested, for many large companies in Berlin and came to Swovatni because he needed a quiet place to work on such serious affairs. He also asked if there were any educated young ladies in the village who might be interested in after-school work and perhaps a bookkeeping apprenticeship.

After a meeting of the village elders, an arrangement was made with the gentleman for the purchase and the building was transferred into his possession. The man seemed extremely well mannered and educated. So, the school principal gave him a short list from the honor roll of young ladies who might meet the position requirements.

After settling into his new office spaces, the bookkeeper held interviews of young ladies on the list and chose three promising candidates for his apprenticeship program.

As it turned out, these young girls would be the very young women that would give birth to the tribe's "beloved triplets".

When the horrid deserters launched their pillage on the village, the bookkeeper secreted his client's files into a small inner pocket of the large cave warren for fear of retribution that might be doled out by his clients if the records got destroyed. He spent most of his time in the cave and had discontinued his apprentice program after the deaths of the mothers of the "triplets". It was during that time that he and Aneya developed a relationship. Though not a native of Swovatni or even someone of gypsy heritage, his need for revenge over the loss of the village, his adopted home, was as strong as hers. So, it was that he offered the aid of his family members who had fled west to avoid the destruction rained on Europe during World War II. They eagerly agreed to provide homes for his and Aneya's sons and protection of the boxes until the boys finished growing up and had homes of their own.

The storage areas for each of the boxes had to always be a priority. Each of Aneya's sons had grown up in a different area of the Western Hemisphere, even the identical twins. However, since it was necessary for her descendants to stay in touch in order to carry on the revenge in the event of the first plan's failure, no one felt the separation would harm them. By the time they left the old country for their new homes, practically everyone in the Western world had home phones at their disposal.

They were all smart boys just like each of their parents and after attending various colleges they landed in different areas of North America, yet still strategically located to inflict the most physical and economic damage. And they were loved by their parents who liked them just the way they were. Aneya never planned any lineal dilution or genetic alterations for her offspring or their descendants. Her dream was that one day the four sons she had sent away, along with their extended families, would be reunited with the three daughters she kept behind in Swovatni and their families. Though she and their father died before her dreams were brought to fruition, she passed still dreaming her revenge and reunion of her family would come true.

The youngest grandsons from Aneya's sons lived in California, Indiana, Florida, and Vancouver. Because of different weather conditions in each region, the families all kept their entrusted cases in various secreted locations. Each had to be in dry moderately tempered enclosures - thus an attic in Florida, a cellar in Indiana, a garage in Vancouver, and a workshop in California. Basements were necessary in the Mid-West where tornadoes scattered household belongings for miles around; garages were carefully constructed to protect much needed auto transportation from unpredictable California earthquakes; summer rains and hurricane threats made attics the most secure storage of family heirlooms in Florida; and workshops carefully guarded tools and weapons needed to survive the Canadian wilderness.

All of these points were carefully kept upmost in the minds of the families entrusted with such lineal responsibility.

The boys' grandmother suspected that the first plan could draw attention by the authorities. Though that plan would definitely give the most immediately gratifying revenge, her ultimate plan would also have a lingering debilitating effect on the Western Hemisphere and their future generations.

The box in a box in a box packaging was necessary because what was contained in the inner most box of each heirloom bin was dormant but still alive and awaiting reactivation.

The small gypsy village had been an agricultural community. It was that fact and its distance from any large city that had made it an attractive hideout for the villainess deserters. Its self-sustainability shielded them for many years until the brave researcher and shaman women were able to make their move.

The work with the fungi went on for years after they regained their tribe's freedom. After developing the spores into weapons to work on humans, other mammals, and avian creatures, the thought arose as to what the spores might do if mixed into the fauna - foliage, fruit, vegetables, and flowers of the countries the Swovatnians hated so much.

So after the "triplets" were sent off, work began on introducing the fungi into various types of seeds, tubers, and pods of vegetation during the development stage. This too took time and effort to accomplish but finally they did.

Aneya had an inquisitive mind that was perfect for the field of research. Having observed not only the psychological effect on the sanity of the original spore carrying bats, but declining mental and physical conditions of later generations, she formulated a further plan of attack.

Whereas the first colony appeared to be focused on eradicating the normal bat residents of the huge cave in order to set up a nesting haven of their own, later generations seemed less and less aware of the need for species preservation or even nest building. They were easily affected by organic elements introduced to their environment causing rashes, loss of fur, and even cancers.

Though changes to a species like that would not produce the immediate devastation of the first spore plan of attack, they could certainly break down the stability of a country by diminishing the quality and productivity of its future generations.

The second instruction for the keepers of the cases was to open the outer box only when it arrived and remove a very small match box and then re-secure the outer box immediately and store the lineal trunks in each ones selected hiding place.

And after successfully adapting the embryonic vegetation to accepting the spores, everything was dehydrated and basically put into suspended life status that could be revitalized later like the seeds that were recovered from the ancient Egyptian pyramids and later grown. In order for this suspension to work, all of the pre-gestational life forms had to remain perfectly and consistently dry and unfrozen. That was why this became the first and foremost order of the commands accompanying the care and handling instructions of the boxes.

Aneya's twin sons in the Mid-West and Southern regions were told to select unguarded working farmland. Her sons on the West Coast and Canada were instructed

115

to select well-travelled highway that sported lush roadside wild flowers. Reassuring them that the tribe had genetic immunity to the fungi and that the immunity would be inherent to their offspring, the boys were told to release the tiny amount of matchbox seeds into the wind over their selected areas.

All of her sons chose fields of medicine and research so that it was easy for them to monitor the results of this small but potentially lethal trial.

Aneya herself died soon after this treacherous trial began. It was neither a pretty nor peaceful death, whether from the evil that was portrayed on her and hers or from the evil that she had grown inside of herself.

The instructions had to be painstakingly hand written by their father since Eric had returned to his life in Berlin after the village regained its freedom. Being a man of degreed letters, he had a clear and concise penmanship which was so necessary for the plan to have any chance of success. He followed the mother of his last brood of children into the ground within months of her succumbing.

It was over thirty years since those test spores were released and it seemed that Aneya's work had hit the mark again. The fungi were reengineered to attach themselves to vegetational embryos in an almost self-grafting way. And it appeared that Aneya's idea of a more indirect and devious method of taking down the enemies of their ancestors may well be the real answer to the Gypsy tribe's half century desire for revenge.

Her sons were doggedly about following changes in life and abilities across the two nations.

They particularly concentrated on the areas east of each dispersal site since weather generally moved west to east and they watched the areas somewhat south of these regions, also.

With statistics at hand for the previous forty years, the brothers were able to document unexplainable swings in allergies; infertility - both in males and females; cancers - in humans and animals; diabetes; autism - mainly in males; asthma - even developing during mid-life; tuberculosis; nervous disorders - ADD and AADD; drug addiction; and even decreasing IQ scores. All fields experienced an increase in occurrences. More and more IQ scores were decreasing and hovering in the average range. It was all ultimately leading to a rise in crime and more people relying on subsistence dependency instead of an honest day's work. Cities were threatening bankruptcy and ignorance was overruling civil diligence.

If this could happen over thirty years at a slow steady pace from such a small sampling, how much more harm could be accomplished with a mass application. They held great faith in the success of the grandsons of Aneya.

The plan for dispersement was in the next step of the instructions since the call from the Elder, who was actually the oldest twin brother, had been received. The cousins had unofficially been tracking the reports of "explainable deaths" in the news, so the calls weren't really a surprise. It was obvious to the cousins that their rolls would have to be called into action. They looked forward to this knowing their duties would be far less dangerous than that of their distant third cousins. The only difficulty foreseen was the part of the instructions that forbad any further communication among themselves. Even living in different regions of the Western Hemisphere, the first cousins stayed in close communication with each other. However, the very things that allowed that close relationship could tie them all together and foil their grandmother's plan.

Each had brought his sacred entrusted container into the house. The second box inside the package contained exact methods for the spore distribution. All of the boys had received their pilot's licenses three years ago and had hundreds of hours in their collective flight logs. The areas for dispersal had been thoroughly scoped out. Each man knew exactly how the wind would affect the spore infused, dried seeds as they were sprayed from the crop dusting rented planes. Of course each plane was rented two to three counties over from the target area under aliases printed on very believable identification obtained from another Gypsy tribe who was expert in that field.

The Swovatni survivors never shared any of their need or plans for revenge with any of the other clans since none of them came to their aid, rescue, or recovery during the village's times of need. As the Swovatnians had to find their own means to survive, so the other tribes would have to fend for themselves along with the luckless descendants of the monsters who caused the revenge to be brought down upon them.

Each of the inner most boxes were packed tighter than anyone could have imagined. The five inch by eight inch by twelve inch box had to contain more than one million small inactive dried pods awaiting activation. The seeds only needed to be tossed on the ground in order to begin gestation once watered. And the first watering after planting on fertile ground would bring that about. So on the eve of the year 2014 Ides of March, just at dusk, the cousins took flight and let the pods fly into the wind that would carry them to their destination of future national devastation. They would be incorporated into fruit, vegetables, and even beautiful flowers that would plant the degrading fungi into the digestive and nasal systems of all living things, peacefully and without warning.

The observations from the aerial test planting proved that this massive aerial planting would surely eventually bring these heartless nations to their knees. It wouldn't happen overnight. It wouldn't happen in 2014. After all, the test brought results over a thirty year period. But the Swovatni Tribe Gypsies will have wreaked their revenge and their heirs may well ultimately be the only ones on Earth sane enough in the next forty years to even realize just what these countries and maybe even the world have lost. After all, air currents don't stop on the east coast and food and flowers are shared around the world.

THE END.....

Lynne Adams Barze' was born in the Treme' area of New Orleans, just outside of the Vieux Carre' where her heritage goes back more than five generations. She began writing when she was ten years old with a poem she wrote to John Glenn whom she later met at a Marine Corps Birthday Ball in the 1980's. She has formerly been a poet and observer of people and life of which she frequently wrote. This is her first novel and her first time delving into this genre. She lives with her husband in Picayune Mississippi and is active in the Picayune Writers Group.

Made in the USA
Columbia, SC
21 September 2022

67143856R00067